# Jimmy and the Secret Letter

**Jim Haskin**

authorHOUSE

*AuthorHouse™*
*1663 Liberty Drive*
*Bloomington, IN 47403*
*www.authorhouse.com*
*Phone: 1-800-839-8640*

*© 2011 Jim Haskin. All rights reserved.*

*No part of this book may be reproduced, stored in a retrieval system, or transmitted by any means without the written permission of the author.*

*First published by AuthorHouse 8/9/2011*

*ISBN: 978-1-4567-1240-2 (sc)*
*ISBN: 978-1-4567-1239-6 (hc)*
*ISBN: 978-1-4567-1241-9 (e)*

*Printed in the United States of America*

*Any people depicted in stock imagery provided by Thinkstock are models, and such images are being used for illustrative purposes only. Certain stock imagery © Thinkstock.*

*This book is printed on acid-free paper.*

*Because of the dynamic nature of the Internet, any web addresses or links contained in this book may have changed since publication and may no longer be valid. The views expressed in this work are solely those of the author and do not necessarily reflect the views of the publisher, and the publisher hereby disclaims any responsibility for them.*

# Other books by Jim Haskin

*Jimmy and the Big Turtle*

CORRECTION: In the last paragraph of the last chapter of 'Jimmy and the Big Turtle' I wrote,

*Union Lake School only offered classes through the fifth grade; Jimmy and his classmates would be the oldest kids in the school.*

When Jimmy completed the fourth grade in 1943 the Union Lake School offered classes through fourth grade. Jimmy and his classmates, like others before them, attended fifth grade classes at the Walled Lake School. The Walled Lake School District added fifth and sixth grade classrooms to the Union Lake School in the 1943-44 school year. The timeline is correct in 'Jimmy and the Secret Letter.' Jimmy is in the fifth grade class at the Walled Lake School, and back at the Union Lake School for the sixth grade.

You may contact Jim Haskin at
www.jimhaskin.books.officelive.com

# Dedication

This book is dedicated to my wife, Alice, and our five daughters, Sheila, Paula, Sharon, Janet, and Julie. Special thanks to Sheila and Alice who helped edit the book.

# Acknowledgement

My best friends in my early years were Ralph Williams, and his two brothers, Joe and Warren (Core). I was unable to contact the Williams family to obtain permission on the use of their names in my first book, *Jimmy and the Big Turtle*. In the book they are referred to as the Clark family and Ralph is called Roger, Joe is named Ron, and Warren is named Don.

The family has given me permission to use their names in 'Jimmy and the Secret Letter'. My best friend in 'Jimmy and the Big Turtle' is named Roger. In 'Jimmy and the Secret Letter' Ralph will rightfully replace Roger. Ralph passed away in 2006.

Photographer Jack Van Coevering took the picture that appears on the back cover of the book the opening day of fishing season, June 24, 1946. Ralph is on the left holding the fish and Jimmy is on the right with his dog King. This is the only picture of the two boys who were thirteen at the time.

# Contents

| | | |
|---|---|---|
| Chapter 1. | March 24th, 1944 | 1 |
| Chapter 2. | The Paper Route | 7 |
| Chapter 3. | Collecting | 11 |
| Chapter 4. | Cleaning the Garage | 15 |
| Chapter 5. | The Trunk | 19 |
| Chapter 6. | Returning the Money | 25 |
| Chapter 7. | Ed Bates Returns | 27 |
| Chapter 8. | The Big Snow | 31 |
| Chapter 9. | Cedar Island Lake | 37 |
| Chapter 10. | The Toad Crisis | 41 |
| Chapter 11. | Opening Day of Fishing Season | 47 |
| Chapter 12. | The Day of Reckoning | 57 |
| Chapter 13. | Later That Week | 71 |
| Chapter 14. | The Stranger | 75 |
| Chapter 15. | Apple Island | 79 |
| Chapter 16. | Exploring the Island | 89 |
| Chapter 17. | Discovery | 97 |
| Chapter 18. | Back to School | 103 |
| Chapter 19. | Surprise, Surprise | 105 |
| Chapter 20. | Next Month | 111 |

## Chapter One

# March 24th, 1944

David jammed himself into the corner under the staircase. He could feel his thumping heart, and his mouth felt dry. The corner was pitch-black, but a crack in the door across the hall painted a narrow stream of light in the hallway. *Please God make them go away. If they find me, they might kill me like they killed the caretaker.* The door in the hall opened, David held his breath, his body motionless. Footsteps on the stairs above him brought him a temporary sigh of relief. A pause followed before a second set of footsteps pounded on the staircase; the man was taking the stairs two at a time. A voice rang out saying, "You take the rooms on the right and I'll take the ones on the left. Let's find that kid and teach him to mind his own business."

"Don't kill him up here! I want him next to the old man

when he dies. We can burn the house down and destroy the evidence."

"Good idea! Let's find him and get out of here."

A paralyzed David heard their plans to kill him. *I was only bringing Mr. Aldrich a piece of cake, and now I'm going to die.* His father wouldn't save him; he hadn't been gone long enough for his father to miss him. He pondered his options, and the ticking seconds seemed like hours. He crouched, biting his lower lip so hard he tasted the salty flavor of his own blood. Tick, tick, tick went the seconds before he realized the value of time, every second counted. The murderers would start looking on the first floor if they didn't find him upstairs. He stumbled from the corner and ran down the hallway to the sewing room. He ripped the curtain from the window frame and frantically tried to open the window, but it wouldn't budge. He grabbed a small chair and hurled it through the window. The four feet to the ground looked liked ten feet and there wasn't time to remove the broken glass. Fear gripped his senses, what to do? He grabbed a cushion from a large chair across the room to cover the window sill. Then he sat on the cushion and swung his legs through the window before dropping to the ground. He had cuts on both hands, but he hadn't broken any bones, or sprained an ankle. He got to his feet and ran toward home.

A murderer shouted, "He's downstairs; I heard a window break."

The other murderer said, "We'll never catch that kid in the dark if he has a head start; let's get out of here."

"Thank you God, thank you so much." David prayed as he ran, but as he neared home he had an unexplainable sense of euphoria not previously felt. What he had experienced at age eleven most people wouldn't experience in a lifetime.

Friday afternoon found the teacher bringing the fifth grade class up to date on the state of World War II. Jimmy sat fidgeting at his desk reliving the story he finished reading last night. He liked reading adventure stories about kids his own age; their lives were exciting ----challenging --- not the old hum drum life at Walled Lake School. He couldn't wait to get home. On Monday, Mr. West from the Pontiac Daily Press called; Jimmy would soon have a paper route. He would be at Jimmy's home today at five o'clock.

The teacher looked at Jimmy staring into space. If he paid attention he would get A's and B's instead of B's and C's. "If it's not too much trouble Jimmy, you might join the class?"

He stammered for a reply, the teacher had startled him.

She raised her voice. "I'm waiting for an answer?"

"I'm-m-m sorry, I'll keep up."

"Maybe repeating the Fifth Grade will make you more attentive. Nothing else seems to work."

The teacher had embarrassed him in front of the class. Being left behind in the fifth grade meant you were really dumb. "I'll pay attention, really I will."

"There's three more months of school and I expect you to do your best."

He nodded his head in agreement. *I'd better pay attention or I'll be in the fifth grade next year with a whole lot of explaining to do.*

Shirley and Marge were giggling and Marge whispered loud enough for several classmates to hear," He'll never learn. Maybe Jimmy is dumb?"

Shirley looked across the aisle at Jimmy to get his attention and snickered, "Big and dumb."

Jimmy muttered under his breath, "I'll get even with those two." Girls were scared of toads. "I'll put toads in their desks." Toads come out in May. "I can wait," he mumbled.

The teacher spoke sternly. "That's enough whispering girls, unless you want extra homework."

Jimmy's best friend Ralph was kidding him on the bus ride home. "You shouldn't talk to yourself, several guys heard you say something about putting toads in Marge and Shirley's desks."

"Not so Ralph, I said those two are dunces. You thought you heard toads."

"There aren't any toads this time of the year. Maybe the other guys will forget what you said, but I don't think so. You should try paying attention in class, you might learn something."

"I'm not the only one who's not paying attention."

"That's right, but you're the only one that gets caught."

"Is it just my imagination----it seems that I get blamed for everything."

"You're the biggest kid and I think these teachers talk to one another. You've been in trouble since the second grade when you put Shirley's pigtail in the inkwell. Stop day dreaming and you'll be okay."

"My dad says that my older brother Hugh and I have to act our height, not our age."

"Being big has its advantages, you're getting a paper route and people think I'm in the third grade."

"It's not fair Ralph, but I read somewhere that life isn't supposed to be fair. Lots of kids are richer than we are. Some kids are smarter and some are good at sports. The lucky ones go to Hollywood and become movie stars."

"Yeah, and we're stuck at Union Lake."

Jimmy and Ralph were the only eleven-year-old boys in the neighborhood. They lived a block apart and had been inseparable since Ralph's family moved to Union Lake three years ago. Ralph had two older sisters, a younger sister Janice, a brother Joe two years older, and a brother Warren (Core) a year younger. The boys played baseball and football together and if a neighbor needed help they would work together. Their classmates referred to Ralph and Jimmy as Mutt and Jeff. The Williams' family was small in height and weight, and Jimmy towered over his friends. They did however make up for their lack of size with quickness and speed that Jimmy couldn't match.

## Chapter Two
# The Paper Route

Mr. West, a man in his fifties arrived promptly at 5 o'clock. He explained to Jimmy that he had started as a carrier at the age of twelve delivering the Detroit Free Press. For the past twenty years he had been a circulation manager for the Pontiac Daily Press. "The newspaper business is what I know, I've been in it all of my working life."

The present carrier planned to quit on March 25th. Jimmy would start his paper route on Monday, March 27th. He wanted Jimmy to deliver papers with the present carrier on Friday and Saturday to learn the route. There were thirty-seven regular subscribers to the afternoon paper and it paid $1.48 a week. The route covered parts of three lakes and the subscribers expected their papers before 6 o'clock. The Pontiac Daily Press didn't publish a Sunday edition and that fit right into Jimmy's schedule. He caddied on Sundays and got to play golf free on Monday mornings during the summer. Mr. West had an agreement that Jimmy and his mother both signed. His mother explained to Mr. West that Jimmy wouldn't be eleven until the 23$^{rd}$ of June. Mr. West said he checked with Mr. Marohn, the shopkeeper, who assured him that Jimmy could handle the route. Mr. West always referred to the customer as the subscriber and the paperboy as the carrier. He handed Jimmy a copy of the contract with a business card. Smiling, he shook Jimmy's hand. "It's a big route Jimmy, but I know you'll do a good job."

"Thank you Mr. West, I'll do my best."

After dinner Jimmy asked his mother for the envelope where he kept his savings. He had saved $29 cutting grass, caddying, raking leaves, shoveling snow and cleaning garages. Twenty-nine dollars represented a substantial amount of money for a ten-year-old and he planned to put it to good use. The new Schwinn bike needed to deliver his route cost twenty-seven dollars. Mother wanted a new dresser set for her toiletries, but he could earn the $5 before Mother's Day. It didn't matter that other kids received an allowance; he didn't mind earning his own money.

There were five in Jimmy's family. His father, a commercial

artist and grandfather, a manager in office services, worked for the Burroughs's Corporation in Detroit. Hugh, his older brother of fifteen, planned to work for his grandfather during summer vacation as a mail boy. Iris, his sister of thirteen, babysat for several families in the neighborhood. The Haskin men were tall, Hugh stood over six feet-three inches, an inch taller than his father. A strong boy for almost eleven, Jimmy had large hands with a tall lean frame. His mother was a stay-at-home mom.

On Saturday morning Jimmy's father and older brother Hugh accompanied him to the bike shop in Keego Harbor. Jimmy wanted the blue and beige Schwinn bike displayed in the window. The salesman adjusted the height of the seat so he could take the bike for a test ride. Jimmy rode the bike in the alley behind the store. Most of his belongings were purchased second hand or handed down from his brother. For the first time in his young life he had something shiny and new. He turned at the corner and headed back to the store. The salesman greeted him, "that's the best set of wheels in town."

"I've had my eye on this bike for weeks."

"It's a good thing you came today; this display model is the last one. From now on the new bikes will be the military type with black paint."

With the new bike, Jimmy could zip around his paper route.

They arrived home to find Ralph there to greet them. He admired the bike and Jimmy lowered the seat so he could take a ride. Six inches shorter, his size prevented him from earning the same money as his friend. If a job required two boys, Jimmy and Ralph would work together cleaning garages in the summer and raking leaves in the fall. Ralph took the bike around the block feeling envious of his bigger friend who happened to be a month younger. Nevertheless, he was happy for Jimmy and hoped for a paper route next year. "It really rides well; I think Schwinn makes the best bikes."

"You'll have a bike before school starts, there'll be plenty of work this summer."

"I hope so. When you're my size, people think you can't get the job done."

## CHAPTER THREE
# Collecting

The first week of April found Jimmy collecting from his subscribers for the first time. Mrs. Jones, a widow in her middle sixties liked to talk. It being Saturday, he had plenty of time to deliver the papers by six. He fumbled for change when she smiled saying, "You can keep the change Jimmy."

He had his first tip. "Thank you Mrs. Jones."

"I live alone, and it's hard to find anyone to do odd jobs. I need my lawn raked and the grass cut every week. You're big and strong, could you do that for me?"

Jimmy wanted more lawns to cut, "I already cut two lawns, but I can do your lawn on Sunday 'til school is out. After that, I can cut it on Thursday morning. I'll rake the lawn tomorrow and cut the grass next Saturday. I charge fifty cents to rake the lawn and fifty cents to cut the grass."

"That will be fine Jimmy. My garage also needs to be cleaned, but I need it done by tomorrow."

"I'll come back this afternoon and rake the lawn. I have a friend who will help me clean the garage. We work together all the time, and we charge a dollar."

"It's pretty messy. I'll pay you $1.50 if you do a good job."

"My friend's name is Ralph. We'll be here tomorrow right after lunch."

Jimmy stopped at Ralph's house on the way home. He and his younger brother, Core, were raking the lawn. Ralph shouted sarcastically, "There's the paper boy."

Jimmy frowned, "A big shot like you doesn't need money. I'll get someone else to help me clean Mrs. Jones' garage. The job pays $1.50, and I'm willing to split the money."

"I was just kidding, I didn't mean it. You know how it is when you say something and then you're sorry. I need to earn some money, really I do. Honest injun, cross my heart and hope to die." Ralph wasn't sure what Jimmy would do next.

"I'll pick you up tomorrow after lunch. Ask Joe if you can use his bike? Mrs. Jones lives on the other side of Cooley Lake."

Core said, "What about me helping, I could use some spending money."

Ralph responded, "Not this time Core, but I'll pay a quarter if you finish raking the lawn."

"That's a deal."

Ralph's older brother Joe worked in the restaurant at the local golf course. "I can use Joe's bike; he gets a ride with one of the cooks. See you tomorrow."

## Chapter Four
# Cleaning the Garage

The boys knocked on Mrs. Jones' door after lunch. She answered the door with a dish of jellybeans. "I thought you boys might want something sweet."

Jimmy introduced Ralph and each took a handful of jellybeans. Jimmy replied, "Thank you ma'am."

Ralph also thanked her.

She smiled, "You're welcome boys. The garage is in the back, let's get started."

The old one car garage needed painting and tilted to one side. Mrs. Jones stared through the dirty window into the dark garage. "I think the light switch is on the right. I doubt if it works! We'll have to use this door; the two swinging doors have a bar that needs to be removed before they'll open." The boys shoved on the side door to make an opening Ralph could squeeze through.

Jimmy said, "Wait a minute a Ralph, I've got a flashlight in my bag." He shined the light through the side window on the garage doors. A large board supported by two brackets sat between the doors. Ralph squeezed through the side door working his way to the larger doors. He removed the board and pushed, but the door didn't budge. With Jimmy pulling from the outside and Ralph pushing from the inside they opened one of the doors. The afternoon sun provided ample light to reveal the mess

"I haven't been in the garage since my husband passed away three years ago. It's a convenient place for my family and friends to store their junk. From the looks of it, there's nothing worth keeping. My neighbor's trailer is behind the garage. Pile all this junk into the trailer and move it inside the garage. He'll take it to the dump on Saturday. That old trunk on the workbench belongs to my daughter's ex-husband. He was a good for nothing bum and the police were after him when he skipped town. My daughter divorced him in 1934 and left the trunk when she moved to Chicago. Take what you want from the trunk; I want no part of it." Mrs. Jones patted Jimmy on the arm. "I'll go make some lemonade. If you boys get thirsty, knock on the door."

Ralph looked at Jimmy with raised eyebrows; this wasn't going to be easy.

Jimmy said, "If there's something that looks good we'll set it outside on the grass and you can decide if you want to keep it."

"That's a good idea, but I doubt if there's anything worth keeping."

Ralph said, "Let's get the trailer. We can start with the boxes."

Jimmy nodded his approval as he put his gloves on. "Give me a hand with the trunk. We'll set it outside and sort through it after we've cleaned the garage."

Mrs. Jones had it right; they found nothing worth keeping. After they finished loading the trailer, Jimmy removed his gloves. "I'm thirsty, let's get some lemonade."

Mrs. Jones met them at the door with lemonade and pretzels. When they finished their snacks she gave each of them three shiny quarters. "I see that you saved the trunk for last. Don't be surprised if it's filled with junk."

The boys, anxious to open the trunk, headed to the garage after thanking Mrs. Jones for the treats.

## Chapter Five
# The Trunk

Ralph ran toward the garage. "Hurry up; I can't wait to see what's in the trunk! I found a crow bar we can use to break the lock."

Jimmy couldn't bust the rusted lock, but the clasp on the trunk that held the lock pulled loose on the second try. He lifted the top backing away from a musty smell that filled the air.

Ralph, anticipating something good, reached into the trunk to remove the top layer of items. Suddenly he jumped back, "Something bit me on the hand."

Jimmy looked in the trunk at a large black spider. "You got bit by a spider. I don't think a black spider can poison you." Jimmy put his gloves on to carefully remove the spider and place it in the garden.

Ralph watched as he rubbed his hand to ease the sting. "I'm

not helping. That smell comes from mold that could make us sick. There's nothing in the trunk that I want."

"A little dust and mold won't hurt you. I'm going to cover my nose and mouth with a handkerchief. That's what the cowboys do in the movies."

"You're gonna look like one of the bad guys in a western. I don't have a handkerchief and you won't need any help."

Jimmy covered his face kneeling beside the trunk. The contents were covered by an old brown newspaper that he carefully removed. He held the paper at an angle brushing away the dust. "This paper is dated 1932; it's older than we are."

"Mrs. Jones said he disappeared years ago."

The first item, a large box, covered the rest of the contents. The box contained an old Army uniform and a packet of photos. Under the large box were items of clothing. The next layer revealed scrapbooks and photo albums. Below the albums sat a pair of shoes next to a metal box.

Ralph commented, "It looks like we struck out. Let's heave that junk in the trailer and go home."

"Wait a minute, there might be something in the box. Hand me the crowbar." The box contained old papers, file folders, and other documents. "Get my bike. I'll toss this stuff in the bag and look at it after dinner. We can dump the rest of it in the trailer."

After dinner, Jimmy got his bag and headed for the basement. His father had made a family work table using an old door set on two wooden saw-horses. Jimmy emptied the bag in the center of the table. The papers were a brownish color and the printing had started to fade. A white envelope wrapped in brown twine caught his eye. It looked like a good place to start. The contents revealed a stack of dollar bills. With a lump in his throat, he remembered Mrs. Jones' words. "Take what you want from the trunk; I want no part of it." And Ralph saying, "There's nothing in the trunk that I want." The bills totaled $75.

The rest of the papers consisted of old letters, a High School Diploma, old photos, and Ed Bates' discharge papers from the Army. The file folders had a bunch of bills and a document from the Oakland County Court. Jimmy didn't understand what some of the papers meant, but they were twenty years old. The last item he opened was a large brown envelope. The contents revealed an old newspaper clipping dated Monday, March 21, 1932. Robbers had stolen $700 from a popular Pontiac restaurant. The crime scene was similar to a robbery in February, where thieves had taken $400 from a different restaurant. The evidence suggested that the robberies were an inside job. Jimmy set the article aside to examine the pictures. One showed two men in uniform, while another picture had the same two men standing behind a bar. They appeared to be working as bartenders. A smaller white envelope had been addressed and stamped, but the flap hadn't been sealed. Jimmy opened the envelope and a letter fell out.

*April 5, 1932*

Tommy

I've got to get out of here, the cops are after me.

They want to play cops and robbers, but I'm not playing.

I'm taking $600.00 and that should get me to California. I put the rest of the money in a box and wrapped it in oil cloth. I buried the box next to the Y-shaped willow tree on the island. When I get settled in California I'll contact you.

Ed

PS I wouldn't touch that money for a while. The cops are questioning my friends, and they'll get to you.

The letter was addressed to, Tommy McMahon
433
Pontiac, Michigan

*Jimmy and the Secret Letter*

Jimmy spoke out loud, "Ed Bates wrote a letter and never mailed it." He examined the envelope. The address didn't have a street. Maybe that's why he didn't mail the letter? If the letter hadn't been mailed, Tommy wouldn't know where to look for the money. Could it still be there? If the police were looking for Ed Bates, he would've stayed in California. Something is missing! Buried treasure stories had a map, and there's no map. Wait a minute! This isn't a story, and I have the only clues to the buried treasure. The article is dated 1932 and it's 1944. He put the letter back in the envelope. *This took place twelve years ago. There's no need to rush. With more time I can figure things out on my own.* He placed the items in a grocery bag and hid the bag in a storage area the family seldom used.

Jimmy lay in bed thinking about his discovery. The other man in the picture must be Tommy McMahon. They worked as bartenders and the article said the robberies were an inside job. Maybe Ed Bates forgot to mail the letter and it got mixed in with the other papers. The letter said he buried the money next to the Y-shaped willow tree on the island. The only island close to Mrs. Jones home is Cedar Island. *If the money is buried on Cedar Island, it's buried in somebody's yard.* Willow trees grew along the shoreline, and there were homes on all the lots facing the water. He had little knowledge of the other lakes near his home, but he knew that only a few of them had an island. Walled Lake School had a library and he could check there on

Monday. He remembered reading a story about robbers hiding money for a fast get away. Maybe that's why Ed Bates put a change of clothes and $75 in the trunk?

He woke up later in the night still thinking of the money. After much deliberation, he murmured under his breath, "I'll give the money to Mrs. Jones when I deliver the paper."

## Chapter Six
# Returning the Money

*Monday* morning Jimmy went to the school library. Only Cedar Island Lake, Wolverine Lake and Orchard Lake had islands large enough to support trees. Cass Lake had a small island that you could see from Commerce Road. He didn't recall seeing any trees on that island, but he could check the next time he went to Keego Harbor.

Later that afternoon Jimmy returned the money to Mrs. Jones. She thanked him for being honest and gave him six-one dollar bills to share with Ralph. Also returned were the photo albums and scrapbooks. He didn't return the letter written by Ed Bates to Tommy McMahon. Mrs. Jones glanced at a picture of the two men dressed in World War I uniforms. "That's Ed Bates on the right with his buddy Tommy McMahon. After Bates disappeared, the police arrested Tommy for robbing a restaurant he and Ed Bates worked at. He claimed to be innocent, but the Judge threw him in jail. The police never recovered the money. I'm sure they robbed the restaurant, but Bates left town before they caught him." She looked Jimmy in the eye, "Choose the right friends Jimmy. A bad apple can spoil the barrel, and if you're not careful, it can spoil you."

On the bus the next morning, Jimmy gave Ralph his share of the reward. The sudden windfall reminded Ralph of Christmas; he'd earned $3.75 since Sunday. "I can't believe there was $75 in the trunk. You did the right thing Jimmy; it wasn't your money." Ralph slapped Jimmy on the arm. "Thank you for sharing, I thought the trunk was full of junk."

"I gave those photo albums and papers to Mrs. Jones. I must have done the right thing, everyone is happy."

## Chapter Seven

# Ed Bates Returns

*Jimmy* seldom read the paper he delivered and most of the headlines were about the war. Local stories that would have normally made the headlines were relegated to the back of the paper. If he or Mrs. Jones had taken time to read the paper they would have seen the small story on page five.

"Detectives working with uniformed officers are still looking for two men who held up a grocery store in Pontiac. Officers interrupted the robbery when they stopped at the store for donuts. The suspect fired three shots that missed the two officers and ran out the rear door with two hundred dollars. He and an accomplice fled the scene in what appeared to be a 1936 Ford four-door-sedan. By the time the officers returned to their patrol car the bandits had made a clean get-away. One of the suspects is identified as Ed Bates. Bates is forty-five years old, five feet ten inches tall, weighs one hundred and seventy-five pounds. He has brown eyes, brown hair and a dark complexion. Bates is wanted in a string of unsolved robberies going back to the early thirties. He and his accomplice are armed and considered to be dangerous. If you have any information regarding the suspect please contact the Pontiac Police."

On Saturday Jimmy knocked on the door and Mrs. Jones answered with a worried look on her face. "You're not going to believe this Jimmy, but I think someone was in the garage last night. I told my neighbor to take a look before he takes the trailer to the dump, and he said all the tools are there and nothing of any value is missing. I want you to take a look; you and Ralph were the last ones in the garage on Sunday."

"I can take a look, but the only thing left that wasn't in the trailer were the garden tools, and some of Mr. Jones tools and tool box."

Jimmy went through the side door and removed the bar from the bigger doors. The garage looked to be the same as he left it on Sunday. "Everything looks the same as it did on Sunday. Probably the raccoons making noise, they come out in the spring."

"Close the doors and I'll get your money for the paper."

"I'll cut the lawn tomorrow if doesn't rain.

Ed Bates had a bad week. The cops were after him in Los Angeles, and he had spent most of his money traveling from California to Michigan. The heist he and his younger brother tried on Tuesday turned out to be a disaster, and now the Pontiac cops were after him. Years ago, his partner in California taught him how to rob a grocery store. "Hook up with a partner who's a car thief and a good driver. Carry an old wallet without identification--- wear a baseball hat, horn-rimmed-glasses and a false mustache. Walk in the store, pick up a couple of items, take out the wallet to pay for them, and grab the money when they open the register. Put the money in a grocery sack and walk out. Do three or four jobs the same night driving a popular model stolen car. When you're finished, wipe the car clean of prints, and dump it across town. I prefer a toy gun, but if you must use a gun, use one loaded with blanks. Robbery carries a two to ten year sentence; murder sends you away for life. If you find it necessary to shoot, fire the gun in the air. The noise will scare everyone including you. If you keep changing disguises the cops will never catch you."

On Tuesday night, he forgot the second wallet so he used his own wallet. When the cops surprised him, he fired live rounds from the gun his idiot brother gave him. In the confusion he dropped the wallet and now the cops had his California

Drivers License. If the cops nabbed him, the rap was robbery and attempted murder.

Ed Bates parked his car a block from Mrs. Jones house. There were clouds overhead and he was wearing dark clothes with a black knit hat. He made his way to the garage behind the house and entered through the side door. He shielded a small flashlight before walking into the trailer and banging his knee. The trunk he was looking for sat on the top of a pile of junk. He placed the trunk on the dirt floor and noticed that the clasp and lock were gone. When he opened the lid, it was obvious that someone had recently gone through the trunk. He emptied the trunk on the dirt floor, but couldn't find the envelope with the money. *Why would that old bat store the trunk for twelve years and go through it the week I come back?* He needed that money to get out of town. After several deep breaths to control his anger, he put the things on the floor back in the trunk and put the trunk back where he had found it. *There's no reason to advertise that I've been here, I still need to get out of town with or without the money. The cops don't take kindly to being shot at and they'll shoot to kill if they corner me. My brother can steal another car and we have enough money to get to Toledo and get jobs in a defense plant. Going straight for a couple of years is better than going to jail or getting whacked by the cops.* He made his way back to the car without being noticed.

## Chapter Eight

# The Big Snow

On Sunday night Jimmy's family gathered around the radio to listen to the popular Jack Benny Program. One of the men who carpooled with Jimmy's father called during the broadcast. "There's two inches of snow on the ground and by morning there could be eight inches. We'll never make it to work tomorrow."

On Monday, Jimmy's father stayed home from work and school was canceled until further notice. Mr. West called; the delivery trucks were equipped with chains and the papers would be there before three. Jimmy knew it would take hours to deliver the papers without a bike, and he couldn't ride his bike in the snow. His father put his hand on his shoulder. "There's a lot of good and a little bit of bad in every job. You'll have to take your sled and walk the route when it snows. Make sure you have a flashlight, it will be getting dark when you reach the Pointe."

Jimmy trudged through the snow on the way to pick up his papers. The snow drifts made it tough going, but today would be a walk in the park compared to what he would face later in the week. Union Lake Village consisted of two grocery stores and a gas station. After picking up his papers at Marohn's Grocery store, his first deliveries were on the North Shore of Cooley Lake. He began the route by walking four blocks north on Union Lake Road to the first subscriber. After delivering six papers, he walked six blocks back to Marohn's and three additional blocks to the next subscriber, the Cooley Lake Inn, on the South Shore of Cooley Lake. The distance wasn't a problem on his bike, but it was half past four and he had thirty more papers to deliver. After Cooley Lake, he delivered the neighborhoods north and east of Long Lake and west of Union Lake. His final deliveries were on the Pointe at Union Lake. The former carrier had warned Jimmy about the last two subscribers. He said they swore at him when he delivered the paper after six and several times they called Mr. West to complain. The roads were covered with deep snowdrifts when Jimmy arrived at the Pointe after six o'clock. True to form, the last two subscribers were angry. One man screamed, "All of you kids are the same, you don't give a X#@X when I get my paper. I don't care how you do it; get my paper here by six!"

No one had ever sworn at Jimmy. "I'm sorry sir. The snow makes it really hard."

"Don't give me excuses. If you can't be here by six, get another kid to help you. The Pontiac Daily Press promises the paper by six and it's up to you to keep their promise."

At half past seven Jimmy sat down for dinner with his brother Hugh. "Mr. Mueller swore at me for delivering his paper after six. He said he called the paper to complain. Will I get in trouble and lose my route?"

"Mr. Mueller swears at all the kids. He gets mad if you walk on his lawn. Mr. West won't take it seriously; he knows Mr. Mueller complains all the time."

"Has he ever sworn at you?"

"Not me, but he swore at Gordon Olson when he had the Detroit News route. He stopped the paper and switched to the Pontiac Daily Press. Just smile and tell him you're doing your best."

Jimmy's spirits improved after their talk and he had another cup of hot cocoa.

School was canceled on Tuesday, and Jimmy faced the same challenge. He arrived at Mr. Mueller's home half past six only to be cursed again! He had been delivering papers for thirteen days, and two of those days had been the worst days of his young life. Tired, he went to bed early. Tomorrow had to be a better day. The weather warmed, but still no school on Wednesday. The snow on the ground created slick spots where the cars had driven. Jimmy tried to avoid those spots, but he slipped and fell several times. After his first delivery, a misty rain began to fall and he could feel a chill running through his body. Halfway through the route, he stopped at home to change shirts and get another jacket.

When he finished the route, Jimmy headed to the warmth of the basement to remove his clothes. King stayed outside shaking his coat. He was part husky and thrived in the snow and cold weather. He hung his wet clothes and jackets on the clothesline closest to the furnace. He would need a dry jacket for school tomorrow.

Thursday morning Jimmy's father went to work and Jimmy went to school. It rained off and on and the ground between the remaining snow drifts and patches of ice turned to mud. He couldn't ride his bike or use the sled. Today, he would carry his papers. After yesterday's experience, his mother purchased a rubber raincoat to protect him from the rain. The coat smelled awful and he hated the dorky matching hat she made him wear.

To protect the papers, he covered them with part of an old inner tube he got from his brother.

    Rain drops were falling as he headed north on Union Lake Road to the first subscriber. Half way through the journey, an oncoming car hit a puddle splashing him with muddy water. The incident repeated it self several times before Jimmy completed his route. Compared to Tuesday, today was shaping up to be the worst day of his life. Another customer on the Pointe yelled at Jimmy when he received his paper after six. In Jimmy's defense, King barked at the man. The man shouted, "Get that @X*# dog off my property and don't bring him back!" Mr. Mueller met Jimmy on the porch to receive his paper; he had already called to complain. Not playing favorites, King barked at him when he shouted expletives at Jimmy.

    Jimmy replied, "I'm doing my best. If you stop swearing and yelling at me, King won't bark at you."

    Mr. Mueller swore again as he retreated into the house.

    Jimmy finished his supper close to bedtime and he hadn't done his homework. His brother Hugh and Gordon were doing their homework. Hugh patted him on the back, "Hang in there little brother, what you're experiencing is part of growing up, but you're experiencing it sooner than most kids. Grownups should know better than to swear at a fifth grade kid who's doing his best."

Gordon said, "Hugh's right! Before the war, thirteen and fourteen year old kids had the paper routes and they were able to sell them when they quit. Every boy wanted to make a couple of dollars delivering papers. I paid $5 for my route and sold it for $7 two years later. Yours is one of the biggest routes in Oakland County and it has the fewest customers. My Detroit News route was half the size of yours and I had forty customers. When the people from Detroit came in the summer I had fifty-five customers. The war has changed everything. Kids your age couldn't get a route before the war."

## Chapter Nine

# Cedar Island Lake

Later in April, Jimmy and his brother were playing catch in the back yard. Jimmy wound up to deliver his best fastball when his mother called from the window, "Jimmy, you have a phone call." A friend who delivered the Detroit News wanted Jimmy to deliver next Sunday's paper so he could go trout fishing with his father. His route began at Cedar Island Lake and ended where Jimmy's route started. He offered thirty-five cents, but Jimmy didn't care about the money. Delivering the paper gave him a reason to be on Cedar Island not once, but twice.

"I can do that. Where should we meet?"

"Meet me Sunday morning at 6:30 at the Cedar Island Store and I'll show you the route. We should finish by nine."

Saturday night Jimmy went to the basement to reread the

letter. "I put the rest of the money in a box and wrapped it in oil cloth. I buried the box on the island next to the Y-shaped willow tree" After Ed Bates disappeared; Tommy went to jail. Mrs. Jones said the money wasn't recovered.

Jimmy rose early to meet his friend Bob at the Cedar Island store. The larger Sunday paper required two bags and a second stop at the store to complete the route. Bob said, "I change deliveries on Sunday so the second trip to pick up the papers is in the middle of the route. Remember to bring an extra bag." They started on the north end of the lake and worked their way to the island. Two narrow dirt roads divided the island with homes on both sides of the street. Bob handed Jimmy a piece of paper. "Here's a list of the homes that receive the paper. Get the homes on that street and I'll get the ones on this street. Please hurry, my family goes to ten o'clock church service."

Jimmy nodded his head. There were no Y-shaped willow trees on his side of the island. On the way back Jimmy observed the tops of several willow trees that were blocked by the homes. He mumbled, "I've waited this long, another week won't matter."

Anxious all week, Jimmy set the alarm clock for six Sunday morning. His heart was racing as he approached Cedar Island; *could this be the day he'd been waiting for?* The homes on the north side of the island shielded the willow trees. The long grass and dirty windows was a sure sign two of the homes were unoccupied summer cottages. After delivering the papers, Jimmy cut between the two vacant cottages and ran to his left toward four willow trees. None of the trees had a Y-shaped trunk. He walked back to the street. There were more willow trees to the right, but the houses blocked his view. He'd delivered their paper and knew the people were home. He retraced his steps between the two vacant cottages and followed the shoreline to the willow trees on the Pointe. The last home had two willow trees and one had been Y-shaped. The branch on the left was intact, but the branch to the right had remnants of a large limb. If a storm damaged the limb, it happened years ago. The partial stump was weathered and rotting from age. *If this is the tree; I can't dig up the lawn, someone will see me.* An older man confronted him as he stood staring at the tree.

"You're up bright and early. Is there something I can help you with?"

The man startled Jimmy; being noticed wasn't part of the plan. He composed himself to reply, "I'm delivering the paper for a friend. He went trout fishing with his father. My class, I mean my teacher, asked us to look for willow trees with a Y-shaped trunk."

"The one on the left used to be Y-shaped. Lightning knocked

part of the branch off in 1927, the year we built the house. My brother is coming next week to help me take it down."

That wasn't the story Jimmy wanted to hear. "It's a very unusual shape. Thank you for helping me."

**"Study hard young man, a good education lasts a lifetime."**

Jimmy finished the route and went to Mrs. Jones' home to cut the grass. He had ample time to think about the letter while pushing the mower. He was down in the mouth and not sure how to proceed in his quest for the buried treasure. In the books he'd read, once you solved the clues you got the treasure. In this book, he had found a Y-shaped willow tree on Cedar Island, but it wasn't the one. The man said the branch fell in 1927. Ed Bates robbed the restaurants and buried the money in 1932.

## Chapter Ten

# The Toad Crisis

On a sunny Saturday in the middle of May, Jimmy pedaled harder to climb the short hill on his way home. He spent the morning cutting two lawns and the afternoon delivering papers. Ralph sat on the front steps waiting to greet him. He looked like the cat that swallowed the canary. He stood up with his hands behind his back, waiting for Jimmy to pet his dog King. "You'll never guess what I found?"

"I'm too tired for a mystery; you'll have to tell me."

Ralph slowly extended his arm revealing a glass jar with two toads. "Lookee, here's a toad for Marge and one for Shirley. You said you would scare them by putting toads in their desks. I can't wait for Monday; maybe the toads will jump on them. Everyone knows that toads pee when they're excited."

"I'm doing better in school, but I'm still on probation.

Fooling around with toads will disrupt the class. The teacher will punish the whole class if no one 'fesses up. If I 'fess up, I won't be promoted to the sixth grade."

"Marge and Shirley called you big and dumb and you said you would get even. Don't tell me you're chicken?"

"I would be big and dumb if I put toads in their desks. When we're mad, we all say things we don't mean. Everyone calls you a runt. Why don't you put toads in all the desks?"

Ralph shuffled his feet attempting to hide his embarrassment. Jimmy's words had left their mark, but he wasn't going to give up. "All the guys know what you said, and they're going to call you a chicken."

"They may call me a chicken behind my back, but they won't say it to my face." Jimmy was searching for something to shut Ralph up. "I get blamed for everything. If you put toads in their desks and don't 'fess up, I could still get the blame."

"This is a really big deal with the other kids! You better make good on your threat, or it's chicken, chicken, chicken."

Ralph had made his point. He'd lose face if he didn't make good on his promise. He paused to consider his options. "I'll do it, but you have to help."

"That's great!" Ralph's enthusiasm was short lived. He didn't want to be part of the prank. "Wait a minute! I'll get a really hard spanking if my father gets a call from the school."

Jimmy wanted a negative response. If Ralph wouldn't help,

he would have to back down. *But then again, with Ralph's help I can pull it off.* "You won't get in trouble if you don't tell the other kids. The Navy says, 'Loose lips sink ships.' If no one knows the plan we won't get caught."

"I'm not going to tell anybody. You know I can keep my mouth shut."

"We'll do it the last day of school, right after the afternoon recess while we're cleaning out our desks. Everyone will be talking and milling about; it won't even disrupt the class. Let's use a couple of grass frogs---- they're really jumpy. I'll put them in their desks, but you have to bring them to school."

Ralph took a moment to consider his role. "Okay! I'll help, but we're going to use toads. The toads will hop on them when they open their desks. Everyone knows if a toad wets on your hand you'll get warts. That's why girls are scared of them."

Jimmy knew the story, but didn't believe it. "You catch the toads and hide them in the room. If you tell someone and I get caught, we both take the blame."

"I'll get the toads in the room and I'm not going to rat you out."

The Allied Forces invaded France on June 6, 1944, and everyone you met talked about the war. On the last day of school, the teacher had borrowed a large wall map to show the class where the fighting was taking place. Ralph had two toads in his lunch box. When the bell rang for afternoon recess, he left the lunch box on his seat. The kids were talking about summer vacation and the confusion allowed Jimmy time to place a toad in each desk. He acted quickly and there were still kids in the room when he left for recess. The last day of school had no planned activity so Jimmy joined some boys who were shooting marbles. Marge and Shirley were skipping rope with the other girls. One could sense the excitement as the children entered the classroom for the last time. The school district had added fifth and sixth grade classrooms to the Union Lake School. Next year Jimmy and his classmates would return to their school for the sixth grade.

The moment of truth had arrived. The girls sat down, lifted their desktops, and screamed when the toads jumped into their laps. The frightened toads jumped again onto their chests causing the girls to swipe at them with their hands. Marge cried out, "Get it off me, I hate toads!" Shirley stumbled from her seat sending the toad to the floor. Just as Ralph predicted, the toad had wet the front of her dress. Most of the kids were standing and the teacher had no idea what was taking place. Luke, sitting across the aisle from Shirley reached for the toad and placed it in his desk. Ralph grabbed the other toad to tuck it away in his desk. Marge yelled, "The toad wet on me." Ralph smiled triumphantly as the kids in the immediate area started to laugh. Shirley and Marge had received their comeuppance.

Luke knew Jimmy had made good on his promise. Abruptly he exclaimed, "The buses are coming fifteen minutes early. We better hurry or we'll miss our bus."

The teacher looked at the clock; the children needed to be out of the room in ten minutes. A boy across the room asked for help, and someone else had a question. Whatever had created the commotion was over.

Marge looked at Jimmy, "You put the toad in my desk and it ruined my dress."

"Why would I put a toad in your desk?"

"I don't know why, but you did it and I'm going to tell the teacher."

An angry Shirley said, "I know you did it. I'm going tell my brother to beat you up."

Shirley's brother was older, but he enjoyed teasing Marge and his sister.

Marge chortled, "You're a big dummy Jimmy and you'll always be a big dummy."

"Sticks and stones may break my bones but names will never hurt me."

Ralph joined the conversation. "What's on the front of your dress Marge? I sit right behind you and I didn't see a toad." He tried to control his laughter, "You better get your stuff Jimmy, our bus is here." The boys left the room as the girls went to the teacher to complain. The teacher listened, but she remembered her last day of school in the fifth grade. A boy constantly teased her for wearing glasses; he called her four eyes. She chewed three sticks of gum to put on his seat the last day of school. "Whatever is on your dresses will come out in the wash. You girls better get packing or you'll miss your bus."

Ralph could hardly stay in his seat on the ride home. Jimmy punched him on the shoulder to remind him about their secret. The other kids had figured it out; there was no need to tell the story.

After the children left, the teacher took time to inspect the desks. When she opened Ralph's desk, much to her surprise, a toad jumped out. She smiled saying, "Boys will be boys."

## Chapter Eleven
# Opening Day of Fishing Season

For Jimmy and Ralph the two most important days in their lives were the opening day of the baseball season followed by the opening day of fishing season. Baseball's opening day had come and gone, but fishing season opened the week after school ended. The boys had access to two lakes. Long Lake had warm shallow water ideal for swimming and catching frogs, but not good for fishing. On the other hand, Union Lake offered cold deep water that harbored large bass, huge Northern Pike, and a variety of pan fish. Jimmy's family docked their boat on the south end of a small bay where the boys liked to fish. The bay had plenty of seaweed along the drop-off that provided an ideal feeding ground for fish and Leatherback Turtles.

Each boy wanted the bragging rights on who would catch the most fish on opening day. When they approached the dock at daybreak, the rising sun from the east and the smooth water combined to paint a perfect image of the willow tree on Union Lake Road. Across the bay, two boats were being launched at the fishing site (public boat launch) interrupting the still of the morning. A large blue heron feeding in the reeds stood between the dock and the willow tree. When a bass jumped, the ripples on the water distorted the idyllic picture. Ralph slapped Jimmy on the shoulder. "Did you see the bass jump?"

"I think he got breakfast. This looks like a good day to fish."

The boys spent yesterday digging worms and catching minnows expecting a record catch. Both bet Ralph's older brother Joe a quarter they would catch twenty-eight fish. However, Ralph neglected to tell Joe or Jimmy about his plan to use two poles. Jimmy asked, "Why do you have two poles?"

"You'll see," Ralph replied as he retrieved the minnows from under the dock. King jumped in the boat and Ralph shoved off as King settled down under a seat. Jimmy rowed to their favorite spot near the willow tree on the edge of the drop-off.

Ralph said, "Let's fish with the worms and night crawlers; we'll use the minnows when we run out of worms."

"Good idea. It worked well last year. I'll bet a Mounds Bar I catch the first fish."

"You're on, but we have to put our lines in the water at the same time. After we catch the first fish we'll use the other pole."

Minutes after they cast their lines, they cried out in unison, "I've got a strike." Both worked hard to land their fish, but the contest ended in a tie. Ralph caught the next fish, a large perch. The extra pole presented a challenge, and each manned the pole if the other was landing a fish. Several times they had three fish on the lines at the same time, making it impossible to determine who caught the most fish. There would be no bragging rights this year. The steady bite provided ample action and they caught thirty fish by noon. The catch consisted of a number of perch and bluegills, but neither boy had caught a bass or a pike.

Grinning from ear to ear, Ralph said, "We've filled both fish stringers and won our bet. Let's clean the fish and have lunch. We can fish for pike after lunch and use our minnows." Jimmy nodded his approval, but he wasn't going to cheat Joe out of a quarter.

Ralph docked the boat while Jimmy put rocks in the two large coffee cans used for the minnows. He placed them under the dock safe from the afternoon sun. Ralph set the two buckets of fish in his red wagon for the journey to Jimmy's backyard and the shade of the maple tree where they cleaned their catch.

Jimmy's mother gave them two pans for the fish with blocks of ice to keep them cool. She also prepared sandwiches for lunch while the boys cleaned the fish. "That's a good catch. Who caught the most fish?"

Ralph replied, "We each caught fifteen fish."

Jimmy said, "That's a record for us."

Neither boy mentioned the use of the third pole---- so they weren't sure who caught the most fish.

"The fish will be a welcome change from macaroni and cheese. I'm going to make some salad and French fries for dinner. That'll taste good with the fish."

"Can you make some tartar sauce? It really tastes good with the perch."

"I sure can Jimmy."

"Can we fish some more this afternoon? We want to catch a pike like Ralph caught last year."

"Be back by two thirty, you have your paper route to deliver."

"Thanks mom, I'll be back by then."

Ralph wanted to fish in the same spot where he caught the pike. He rowed the boat in a circle to select the perfect location.

His hands were smaller and he carefully baited Jimmy's hook. A properly hooked minnow would continue to swim and attract the pike. Jimmy adjusted his bobber to the new depth before dropping his line into the water.

Ralph had an eager look about him when he put his line in the water. "I'm going to catch another pike Jimmy; I can feel it in my bones."

"Last summer we fished the whole lake and we never caught another pike."

"That was last year. I'm lucky on opening day, you'll see."

Ten minutes later Ralph checked his bait. The minnow was dead. He changed the minnows every ten minutes, but neither pole fetched a strike.

Ralph used the last two minnows and they placed their lines in the water. Jimmy shouted, "I got a strike! Get the net, it feels like a big fish."

Ralph looked every where, but he couldn't find the net. "We left the net on the dock."

"I'm not sure what I hooked, but it doesn't feel right. It's heavy like a bass, but the fish isn't moving." The line slackened and Jimmy couldn't feel the fish. It took forever to wind the line around the tip of the pole until it went past the bobber. He shortened his reach while raising the pole. A Leatherback Turtle appeared with the line coming out of its mouth. Jimmy had caught a small Leatherback two years ago, but this one looked to be ten inches in diameter.

Ralph shook his head. "I'm not fooling with that turtle. Get him close to the boat so I can cut the line."

"No way, Mr. Marohn says Leatherbacks make good turtle soup. I bet my brother could clean it like he does the rabbits he shoots. Take the pole and I'll pull the line with my hands." Jimmy brought his leather work gloves to handle the sharp teeth if he caught a pike. He donned the gloves and slowly pulled the line toward the boat. The helpless turtle offered little resistance and Jimmy placed it in the pail. Not liking captivity, the Leatherback made a screeching sound as it clawed the sides of the metal pail trying to escape.

Ralph said. "That turtle is small compared to the one we tried to catch last summer. It's like comparing King Kong to a monkey."

"Leatherbacks are easy to handle if they're hooked. This one is big enough to make a pot of soup."

"We better get going. It's close to three, and you have your paper route"

They headed to Ralph's house after docking the boat. Joe and little sister Janice stood waiting for them at the top of the driveway. "Mom said you caught thirty fish. Are you putting me on?"

"You can ask Jimmy's mother. She divided the fish."

Joe liked to kid around with Ralph as he reached into his pocket for some change. When he handed Ralph the quarter, Jimmy said, "We used three poles, we cheated."

Ralph gave Joe a sheepish look and returned the quarter. "You don't owe me a quarter, I owe you a quarter. Using three poles was my idea. We had a good chance to win the bet without cheating."

Jimmy reached into his pocket for a quarter. "I think we caught eight fish on the extra pole, but I'm not sure."

Ralph yelled, "I want a chance to get my money back. We'll go fishing again on Monday if the bet is twenty-seven fish."

Joe shook his head, "Twenty-seven is too easy. Let's make the bet twenty-nine. Jimmy said you caught twenty-two fish with two poles."

Ralph extended his hand. "We can catch twenty-seven fish. Is it a bet?"

"You're a sucker Ralph. Are you in for a quarter Jimmy?"

Jimmy had second thoughts, but he wasn't a chicken. "It's a bet." Jimmy reached to shake Joe's hand when Ralph blurted out, "Double or nothing. Let's make the bet double or nothing. I want a chance to make some real money."

"You're crazy Ralph. The bet is a quarter."

"It's a bet. Fifty cents you don't catch twenty-seven fish on two poles." He turned toward Jimmy, "Are you in Jimmy, or are you a chicken?"

Jimmy wanted no part of fifty cents, but no one called him a chicken.

Ralph stared at him. "Jimmy's no chicken. He's in for fifty cents."

"I'm no chicken. It's a bet."

Ralph glared at his brother. "You're going to owe us a dollar Monday afternoon. Just you wait and see."

"You have 'til three o'clock Monday afternoon to catch twenty-seven fish on two poles and they have to be keepers. You can't throw in little bluegills or perch."

Ralph walked over to his brother and tapped him on the chest. "We know the rules."

Janice looked in the pail. "What are you going to do with the turtle Jimmy?"

"Mr. Marohn said that Leatherbacks make good soup."

"That's gross, I wouldn't eat it."

"That makes two of us. It's bad enough having to eat fish. I like hamburgers with lots of ketchup and fried onions," Ralph retorted.

Joe said, "You'll never catch the Williams' family eating a turtle. They crawl around on the bottom and eat dead fish."

"I've got papers to deliver. We'll need some worms and the privilege lot on Union Lake is all dug up."

"Tomorrow we can dig for worms at the privilege lot on Long Lake. I'll bring my wagon and the minnow net."

After dinner, Hugh said he would clean the turtle. The Leatherback, sensing danger, retreated to the safety of its shell. Jimmy held the turtle while Hugh used the line from the turtle's mouth to pull the head out. He grabbed his hatchet, off came the head. He turned the turtle on its back and used the hatchet to split the shell. The whole thing bothered Jimmy and he turned away when his brother split the shell. "I could never do that!"

"Every time you clean a fish you do it! Not all creatures are the same, but you have to gut them to eat them."

"I guess you're right, but a turtle or a rabbit seem more alive than a fish."

Hugh did a good job cleaning the turtle and gave his mother a sizeable amount of edible meat. Mom had a recipe for turtle soup she got from a neighbor. On Sunday the family dined on salad greens, turtle soup, homemade bread and fish for dinner. They were all tentative about eating the pieces of turtle meat in the soup. Jimmy's father took the first bite. After faking a grimace he said, "Go ahead; turtle is no different than rabbit."

## Chapter Twelve

# The Day of Reckoning

On a cold and wet Monday morning, a storm was building from the Northwest. Jimmy and Ralph didn't fish in bad weather; they went back to bed and waited for a sunny day. As he dressed, Jimmy walked about talking to himself. "The bet is about catching the fish today, so I can't go back to bed. We've never fished in the rain, nobody fishes in the rain; I'll need my raincoat to stay dry and I'm going to smell like an old tire." Ralph and Joe were waiting under the maple tree when he showed up.

"Why don't you give me the fifty cents and go back to bed? You won't catch any fish in this weather."

Jimmy whined, "Its not fair Joe. Nobody talked about rain. It'll be a fair bet if we fish on Wednesday."

"Ralph said you'd catch the fish on Monday. Today is Monday and that's why I'm up early. The restaurant is serving a ladies breakfast and I need to help. I'll see you suckers this afternoon when we count the fish. If you want to try again on Wednesday, let's make the bet a dollar so you can win your money back." Joe started laughing as he rode down the driveway on his bike. After reaching the street, he turned his head and shouted, "You two better get going, you're wasting time."

As Joe disappeared from sight, Jimmy felt drops of rain striking his head. He gave Ralph a determined look. "I'm not giving up. Only the fish know if they're going to bite."

"I'm no quitter! Let's catch those fish and we can rub Joe's nose in their guts." Ralph started down the driveway pulling his red wagon. He looked ridiculous in a slicker and boots that were two sizes too big, but that's how clothes got handed down in a large family.

On the way to the dock, drops of icy rain combined with small hail, rained down on their backs. On Sunday afternoon Jimmy put the twenty minnows they caught on Long Lake in two coffee cans and placed them under the dock. He grabbed a can and was shocked to find dead minnows floating on top of the water. "There's a bunch of dead minnows, and the live ones don't look too good. They're in the same place I always put them and the water is running through the holes."

"Maybe the minnows we caught at Long Lake don't like Union Lake. This is bad Jimmy, really bad. Those other minnows won't last 'til noon. We're gonna have to use them first thing."

"I think you're right. We'll have to fish in the new spot to use the minnows. If we don't catch any perch, it'll be after seven before we start fishing with the worms." Jimmy looked worried, "What should we do?"

Ralph paced back and forth on the small dock before speaking. "Maybe we should save our worms for Wednesday and bet Joe another fifty cents. I'm all sweaty inside this stupid slicker and my hands are cold."

"We can dig worms and catch more minnows if we're going to fish on Wednesday. Let's try the new spot and use the minnows. We'll be plenty warm if we're catching fish. It's no different than playing hockey on a cold day. You're not cold if you're doing something."

Ralph chewed on his lower lip. "Okay! Get in the boat and I'll shove off."

Jimmy headed for the spot where he thought the perch would be. "There are ten minnows left. You can use the minnows; you're better at hooking them. I'll use the worms and fish for rock bass and bluegills; they're all over the lake."

"Good idea! I read in 'Field and Stream' that perch will bite on dead minnows if they're really hungry. I'll bet a Mounds bar I catch the first fish."

Jimmy stopped the boat. "That's a bet! I think this is the place, drop the anchor."

As Jimmy dropped his line in the water, thunder roared from the west side of the lake, accompanied by high winds and heavy rain. Where there was thunder, there was lightning, and the boys knew they shouldn't be on the lake. When the first bolt of lighting flashed near the north shore, he knew to head for the dock. Jimmy yelled at Ralph, as a bolt of lightning thundered to the east, "This looks like a really bad storm. We better head back to the dock."

Ralph grabbed the anchor. "If lightning hits the boat we're goners."

As Jimmy pulled on the oars, he heard more thunder and lightning at his back. Try as he may, he couldn't make any headway against the wind and high waves. The small plywood boat had a flat bottom that acted like a sail when it crested on top of an oncoming wave.

"You have to row harder Jimmy, we're moving away from the dock."

"I'm rowing as hard as I can. The wind blows the boat

backward every time it hits a wave. I'm going to turn the boat around and head toward the Pointe. We can dock there while we wait out the storm."

"We have to get off the water. I never told you, but I'm scared of thunder and lightning. Our moms will be waiting for us at the dock. We can't go to the Pointe."

"There's a small swimming area next to the cottage with the green shutters---if we're lucky we can beach the boat there, I can't get back to the dock." Before Jimmy finished his sentence, lightning struck a tree near the cottage with the green shutters.

Ralph looked terrified. "There are high banks on both sides of that beach, go to the blue house."

"My grandfather told me, 'Lightning never strikes twice in the same place.' If I try to go to the blue house, the wind will take us to the other house. I can't row against the wind."

When Jimmy turned the boat, a large wave washed over the side dumping water into the small craft. The added weight of the water and the big waves made the boat hard to handle. Jimmy yelled, "Get the water out of the boat or we'll tip over." Ralph threw the minnows overboard and used the pail to bail the boat. In the confusion his bamboo pole disappeared over the side. "Keep bailing Ralph, we can buy another pole."

Jimmy now had his back to the Pointe and he turned to face the cottage with the green shutters. He didn't need to row; with the winds help, the small boat was surfing on top of the waves. As they neared the shore Jimmy said, "The water is deep along those steep banks, if we miss the beach, be ready to jump on the bank so we can get the boat out of the water." Ralph kneeled on the front seat and grabbed both sides of the boat as he readied for action. "I think we'll make it," Jimmy yelled as he pushed on the left oar to steer the boat. Ten feet from the shore a sudden gust of wind accompanied by a large wave changed their course and slammed the boat against the bank pitching Ralph out of the boat. Not prepared for the change in direction the sudden stop tossed Jimmy forward striking his head on the edge of the seat Ralph had vacated. The blow caused him to lose consciousness for a short time and when his eyes opened he could taste blood mixed with rain running down his face. The blow to his forehead opened a surface cut. He lost his balance when he tried to stand and fell backwards on the middle seat.

Ralph hit the ground hard jamming his wrist. He rubbed the wrist and rolled over as his friend tried to right himself. "What happened? I thought we would make the beach. You cut your forehead, it's really bleeding."

A dazed Jimmy swiped at his face. "That darn wave took the boat the other way. I can taste blood. Are you all right?"

"I think so! I'll help you out of the boat. We need to stop the bleeding."

Jimmy's backward fall changed the balance of the boat and a wave carried it atop a steep two foot bank halfway out of the water. The incoming waves threatened the little boat and Ralph knew that it could break up if left in the water. It tipped from side to side as Jimmy tried to regain his balance. Ralph took his boots off and waded into neck high water to steady the boat and help his buddy to solid ground. After he got Jimmy to the shore, it took all of his strength to pull the boat to the safety of the beach. Jimmy wanted to help, but standing up made him dizzy and he felt like throwing up. The ever increasing gusts of wind were blowing the rain almost sideways and he wobbled in his boots full of water trying to keep his balance. A nearby willow tree with a beached boat tied to it offered some shelter. Ralph came to help him, "Put your hand on my shoulder and we can get to the willow tree and take your boots off."

"Okay!

Blood was streaming down Jimmy's face as Ralph removed his boots.

"Lie down next to the boat and I'll use my handkerchief to apply pressure on the cut. My mother says that's the best way to stop the bleeding."

Jimmy felt dizzy as Ralph pushed down on the cut. He had

trouble focusing his eyes. Without warning, his body started to shake from the cold and hitting his head.

Jimmy's eyes looked funny, and the shaking concerned Ralph. "Put your hand on the handkerchief and press down on the cut. Does this house get a paper?"

"These---these are summer---summer cottages, there's---there's no one here."

"We need to get help. Does your mother have the car this week?"

"She—she has the car---car---car and my-my sister is home. I can walk---walk---walk home---home after the storm lets---lets up."

"When your head hit the seat it sounded like a fire cracker. Football players wear helmets and they get concussions when they hit their head. I don't think you should walk. I'm going for your mother, she knows about this stuff. Keep the handkerchief on the cut and don't try to stand up. I promise to be back in thirty minutes."

"Hurry up---up, I'm getting cold---cold."

Jimmy's mother had finished the morning dishes when thunder and lighting shook the house. She wasn't concerned; Jimmy and Ralph knew to head for the dock or the fishing site during a storm. Ten minutes later Ralph's mother called to ask if the boys were at her house. "I walked down to the dock.

The boat isn't there, and they aren't fishing in the bay. I looked toward the far shore and there isn't a boat on the lake. I'm really concerned. It's a small boat and the waves and wind are stronger than ever."

"We're not going to find the boys without some help. Mr. Robinson works afternoons and he should be awake by now. He knows the lake and where to look."

"He doesn't like children, Ralph says he ignores him."

"Jimmy delivers his paper and he says Mr. Robinson is nice once you get to know him. He's the only man I know that's not at work. If the boat has turned over the boys will need help. I'll go to the house and ask him in person."

Ralph's mother replied, "That's a good idea, but please hurry, I'll be waiting for you at the dock."

She woke Jimmy's sister Iris, and told her she needed Mr. Robinson's help to look for Jimmy. Iris nodded as her mother donned her coat and headed for the door. She half ran the block to the Robinson home and breathed a sigh of relief when he answered the door.

"Good morning, I'm sorry to trouble you. Jimmy and Ralph left early this morning to go fishing. Mrs. Williams went to the privilege lot to check on them when she heard the thunder. She's concerned, the boys aren't in the bay where they normally fish and there are no boats on the lake." She wiped at the tears forming in her eyes. "We're worried and we don't know what to do!"

He sensed her anxiety, and she had good reason to be concerned about her son. Jimmy's little boat could be capsized in the wind and big waves. Remaining calm he said, "I'll go look for the boys. Come inside while I get my raincoat and tell my wife where I'm going. The motor is in the garage and we can take my car."

Ralph lowered his head, the rain and occasional hail accompanied by gusts of wind made it hard to see, and the oversized boots and slicker made it difficult to run. After falling a second time, he discarded them in the grass along the road and ran the remaining two blocks on bare feet. Jimmy's sister babysat Sunday night and not sensing the need for immediate action, rolled over and went back to sleep. *What's new, Jimmy and Ralph were missing.* Ralph pounded on the door for what seemed like an eternity before a sleepy-eyed Iris responded. He stood on the porch, shivering in the icy rain before she realized he needed help. She handed him one of Jimmy's sweatshirts and a towel as he headed to the bathroom to change clothes.

Ralph came out of the bathroom with the sweatshirt down to his knees and asked what they were doing to help Jimmy? Iris explained that her mother had gone to ask Mr. Robinson for help, and he responded, "They won't find him on the lake. I left Jimmy at the Pointe to come for help. I'll go to the privilege lot and get your mother and Mr. Robinson. You can't see the cottage from the street and they'll need me to find it."

Ralph's feet were sore, but he quickly covered the short distance and arrived at the privilege lot as Mr. Robinson started the motor. Gasping for breath, he explained what had happened. Mr. Robinson and their mothers were relieved that they weren't in the water, but thirty minutes had elapsed since he left Jimmy under the tree. Mr. Robinson turned off the motor and suggested they go by car to rescue Jimmy.

Jimmy shivered from the cold and felt dizzy trying to keep pressure on the cut. He tried to stay awake, but his body wanted rest, and he drifted off into a heavy sleep. In his dream he was hiding behind a bush at the fishing site waiting to catch the big Leatherback Turtle. His heart beat faster when a large Leatherback came out of the water to rest beside the willow tree while enjoying the morning sun. Could this be the day he would catch the big turtle? While waiting for the turtle to fall asleep, a second turtle larger than the first one emerged from the water, followed by another large turtle. Which one was the real big turtle? What difference did it make? Any big turtle would do. Springing to action from behind the bush, he charged the turtles at full speed. When he looked into the eyes of the closest turtle, it seemed to be laughing and moving backwards. He stumbled forward losing a shoe and fell face-first into the shallow water. When he looked up, the turtles were moving toward him. The big turtles weren't laughing, they looked angry. He tried to crawl away on his hands and knees, but an angry turtle reached out with her flipper and scratched his leg. He looked over his shoulder and screamed when a second turtle bit him on the heel. "Get them off me, get them off me!"

"Wake up Jimmy, you're dreaming." He woke to see a shivering Ralph standing beside his mother dressed in his Detroit Tiger's sweatshirt while she covered him with a blanket. He didn't remember the storm or hitting his head. The dream had been so real, he thought his leg hurt, not his head.

"Why are you here---here and why is Ralph wearing my--my Tiger's sweatshirt?"

Ralph said, "You hit your head when the boat hit the bank. We needed help, so I went to get your mother. My clothes were wet and Iris gave me your sweatshirt. Lick your lips and you'll taste blood."

Jimmy licked his lip and tasted the blood. That's why his head hurt. "Oh yeah, now---now I remember. Where's the—the---the boat?"

His mother said, "The boat's on the beach and we need to get you to the doctor."

Mr. Robinson wrapped Jimmy in the blanket and helped him into the car." He's ice-cold and suffering from shock. It could be a concussion, but the doctor will know." He turned to Ralph, "You boys are lucky to survive. This is the worst storm in my twenty-five years at Union Lake. You wouldn't have lasted twenty minutes in the waves and cold water if the boat had capsized." He pulled the boat ten feet from the water and threw the anchor on the beach. "We'll fetch the boat after the storm clears."

## Chapter Thirteen

# Later That Week

Ralph and Jimmy's mother delivered the papers on Monday, and Ralph agreed to deliver the route the rest of week. Jimmy had sustained a concussion and the doctor told him to take it easy. Joe and Ralph were concerned for their friend, and visited with him on Wednesday. Joe spoke as they were leaving, "I can't take your fifty cents Jimmy, I'm calling the bet off. You can try again if you're game."

Ralph quickly added, "Jimmy's no chicken, we'll try again!"

"I'm game for another fifty cents."

Saturday afternoon Jimmy and Mrs. Jones were sitting on the porch having milk and cookies while she explained the need to wear a life jacket. She had heard the story from Ralph when he delivered the paper. To protect his head while riding his bike, Jimmy was wearing a football helmet that his brother borrowed from a friend. "If you were my grandson, I would make you wear a life jacket!"

"I don't want to wear a life jacket. Ralph and I are good swimmers, and we're not going to drown. I hit my head when the boat hit the bank."

"I can see you're not going to follow my advice, but please wear the helmet when you're riding the bike. I need my paper delivered and someone to do the chores. Ralph needs to grow some to replace you."

"Thank you for the milk and cookies. I'll cut the lawn tomorrow."

"Before you go, come see the garage. My neighbor built shelves out of some old lumber and I put most things in boxes. Now I can find what I'm using."

The difference shelving had made surprised him when he entered the garage. It also brought back memories of the trunk. He remembered Ralph getting bit by the spider and the night he read the letter. He had fun fishing, but he needed to renew his effort to find the island and the Y-shaped willow tree. The map at school showed two islands on Wolverine Lake, but Jimmy doubted if they were large enough to support trees.

Apple Island, located in Orchard Lake was the largest island in Oakland County.

Jimmy stopped at Ralph's house on the way home. Joe greeted him. "It looks like you've recovered. If you still want to lose fifty cents, you can try again next week."

Joe thought he had a couple of losers, and Jimmy wasn't sure if he could change the lake and the rules. "I hear there's lots of big bass in Orchard Lake. I'll bet fifty cents that Ralph and I can catch two bass in Orchard Lake."

Joe laughed, "You guys have never caught two bass the same day in any lake; that's a bet."

Ralph came out of the house, "Joe wants to bet again."

"I bet fifty cents we'd catch two bass in Orchard Lake."

"We've never fished in Orchard Lake and bass are hard to catch."

"We'll go after the Fourth of July. Mr. Marohn says that everybody catches bass in Orchard Lake." Jimmy needed to convince Ralph.

"Who's going to pay for the boat? The rental is $1.50 a day."

"I'll pay for the boat."

Ralph took a minute to contemplate. "It would be fun to fish in a different lake. I'll bet fifty cents we can catch two bass."

Joe responded, "How about a dollar, do you want double or nothing?"

"I'm betting fifty cents, but Ralph can bet more."

Ralph had some extra money from delivering Jimmy's route and cutting lawns last week. He gave Joe a cursory look. "Okay! Okay! I'll bet a dollar, but you're going to lose."

"I only make thirty-five cents an hour. Betting with the two of you is better than working."

## Chapter Fourteen

# The Stranger

On Saturday afternoon Mrs. Jones had finished lunch when she heard a knock at the door. *It's probably Jimmy collecting for the paper,* as she reached for her purse. She opened the door to be greeted by a short stocky man in his forties who looked vaguely familiar.

"Remember me? I'm Tommy Mc Mahon!" Before she could respond, he asked, "Have you seen anything of Ed Bates? I haven't been able to contact him since I got out of jail."

Tommy was the last person she wanted to talk with. "Check the jails in California, they probably can find him. He left Michigan years ago."

"A friend said he went to California. He also said Ed tried to rob a grocery store in Pontiac back in April. If he came here all the way from California, I'm surprised he didn't pick up his trunk. Are you sure he wasn't here?"

Mrs. Jones thought, now is the time to get even with Bates and Tommy. "My daughter moved to Chicago after she divorced that good for nothing bum and left the trunk in my garage. I cleaned the garage in April and threw out the trunk. The only things worth keeping were the pictures of my daughter. If Ed Bates showed up here, I'd have him arrested."

Tommy frowned and went on talking. "He had a pretty good trunk. Why would you throw it away?"

"See here Tommy, I stored that trunk for twelve years. Ed Bates never claimed it and you were in jail for robbing restaurants. What I did with the trunk is none of your business, and I'm through talking about it."

"Ed Bates and one of the cooks robbed those restaurants, it wasn't me. I know Ed left money someplace, and some of that money is mine."

"If you didn't rob the restaurants, why on earth did they put you in jail?" Mrs. Jones looked flustered trying to cope with the situation.

Tommy noticed that she was uncomfortable and fumbling her words when he asked a direct question. "There's something fishy going on. I know when someone is lying; I've spent the last twelve years with liars."

Mrs. Jones sensed that she wasn't a good liar. "You were

the smarter of the two. And you're right about the money; we found $75 in the trunk." She opened her purse to hand thirty dollars to Tommy. "This is more than you're entitled to. Now leave before I call the police."

Tommy pocketed the money and he spoke softly. "No problem, I know it's hard for old people to remember. I'm trying to make a new start and I've been offered a job in Florida working in a citrus orchard. I'm really sorry for the way I acted. It's hard to give up old habits that you learned in jail." He hung his head. "You were right; Ed and me robbed those restaurants and two or three gas stations. He left town with the money before I got my half. I've learned my lesson and paid my debt to society. I'd be happy if I never saw Ed Bates again. I got $50 from my sister and the man in Florida sent me another fifty. With the money you gave me I can make the trip. Thank you so much for your help. I hope there are no hard feelings." He extended his hand to Mrs. Jones.

She felt moved by his change of manner and opened her purse. "Here's another twenty dollars, you'll need to eat something along the way. I'll pray for a safe journey and your new job. Please tell me you're not going to make the trip in that old car?"

"No ma'am. I borrowed the car from my sister to come here. Greyhound has a bus running from Detroit to Lakeland,

Florida once a week. The orchard is in Frostproof, about twenty-five miles from Lakeland."

"You might consider joining a church in Frostproof."

"I will. The man I'll be working for is a deacon in the church." He took a handkerchief to wipe a tear from his eye. "Please forgive my behavior. It's been hard to leave prison life behind me and I'm still learning to control my temper. I don't have many friends I can trust. If you don't mind, I'll drop you a post card from time to time and let you know how things are going."

"I would appreciate that, and God Bless."

"Thank you so much for your understanding."

Jimmy saw a man get into an old Chevrolet Car when he turned into Mrs. Jones' driveway. The man waved as he pulled away from the house. Mrs. Jones stayed on the porch with her purse in hand. He handed her the paper and she opened the purse and gave him thirty-five cents. "Keep the change."

"Thank you Mrs. Jones, I'll be on my way." He was running late and thankful that she didn't want to talk.

After Jimmy left, she sat down and breathed a sigh of relief. Thank God Jimmy came after Tommy left. There was no need to involve him with Tommy McMahon and Ed Bates, and their sordid past. *I feel better with the truth and the money will be better used if it helps Tommy turn a new page in his life.*

## Chapter Fifteen
# Apple Island

Jimmy wanted to check the islands in Wolverine Lake before venturing to Orchard Lake to explore Apple Island. Fortunately, a classmate lived on Wolverine Lake. Saturday morning they explored the two islands with trees. The willow trees had been dead for years, and they weren't Y-shaped. His friend remarked that he and his brother trapped muskrats in the fall. He showed Jimmy several holes in the banks that the muskrats used for shelter. Jimmy asked, "How much do you get for a muskrat pelt?"

"Fifty cents for most of them, but the real big ones are worth a dollar. Have you ever eaten muskrat? My mother makes muskrat stew with lots of onions, carrots, and potatoes. It's pretty good."

"Isn't a muskrat just a big rat that lives in the water?"

"It's a big rat, but people in poor countries eat rats. It's no different than venison or wild duck; they're all kind of gamey. Meat is rationed and my dad says it doesn't make any sense to throw it away. I'll give you a couple this fall when we start trapping."

His friend was right. When there weren't any fish or frog legs to eat during the winter months, Jimmy's family was eating macaroni and cheese three nights a week. They would welcome some muskrat stew.

Jimmy had visited the school library to read about Apple Island. The thirty-five acre island was the largest island in Oakland County. Historians claimed Chief Pontiac spent time on Apple Island and the surrounding shores in the 1760's, but there were no written records. The island stood in the middle of Orchard Lake, a good distance from the nearest shore. It had a sufficient number of trees for firewood, lots of deer, and the lake had an ample supply of fish. To an Indian Chief, Apple Island offered the security of a fort with a large moat, the ideal place to spend the summer months. In the late 1800's and the early 1900's a dairy farm occupied the island. The family left the island in 1920 when fire destroyed their house. Now, private property, the owner had posted 'NO TREPASSING' signs. A boat livery on Orchard Lake Road sold bait and rented boats for $1.50 a day.

Mr. Marohn told Ralph that Orchard Lake had lots of bass and the expectation of catching one excited him. Ralph wanted to fish with night crawlers and it took three nights to catch ten of them with the help of his sister Janice. Mr. Marohn said to fish with a spinner and a medium sized hook. "Put the spinner about an inch above the hook and bait the hook with half of a night crawler. Move the line up and down and the spinner will attract the fish. You don't need a bobber, but make sure you're not on the bottom. You can fish wherever there's scattered weeds. Orchard Lake doesn't have a drop-off."

As part of the plan, Jimmy's father would drop their bamboo poles and tackle box at the Boat Livery on the way to work and pick them up on the way home. The boys waited for the morning traffic to clear before embarking on the four-mile bike trip. Ralph was eager to go fishing and Jimmy worked to stay up with him on the ride to Orchard Lake. To make sure there were no willow trees on the small island in Cass Lake, Jimmy stopped where Commerce Road separated Orchard Lake and Cass Lake by a hundred feet. There were no willow trees on the island. Ralph complained, "Come on Jimmy, we're almost there."

When Jimmy rented the boat, the man at the boat rental charged him a dollar for two life jackets he insisted they wear.

He promised to give Jimmy a fifty-cent refund if they returned the life jackets in good condition.

"We're good swimmers and we never wear life jackets." Ralph reminded his friend.

Jimmy wasn't going to complain. He remembered getting knocked out in the storm.

"I don't care what you do on your own. When you're in my boat you wear a life jacket. If I see you're not wearing them, I'll come and get you myself."

Orchard Lake varied in depth from ten to thirty feet. He suggested they fish on the northeast side of the island about two hundred feet from shore. As they were pushing off, the man said, "Stay off the island, its private property."

Ralph remarked, "This is great, I can't wait to catch the first bass."

As Jimmy pulled on the oars, he had a good view of the hill overlooking the boat livery that separated Orchard Lake and Pine Lake. In the 1700's it would have been straight down a one hundred foot rocky bluff to Orchard Lake. With water on two sides, the hill would have been easy to defend and maybe that's where the Indians built their tepees. Years ago the railroad had removed part of the steep bluff above Orchard Lake Road to build the track connecting Wixom with Pontiac. As Jimmy took time to reflect, the morning train blew its whistle at the crossing and smoke curled up from the engine that was barely visible from the lake.

Ralph said, "Wow, what a sight. Can you imagine what this looked like before the settlers got here? This is like the North Shore of Union Lake, but much steeper. When you're riding in the car it doesn't look the same."

"The lakes are so close together the Indians could have carried their canoes."

"The correct term is 'Portage' Jimmy. I read that in, 'The Last of the Mohicans.' The word means to carry goods from one waterway to another. When the Indians were here, they used their canoes like we use trucks. The Mohicans lived in the Northeast where there are many lakes and rivers."

"If you took away the train and the road, this area hasn't changed that much." Jimmy didn't know what to expect when he explored the island, but he wanted to climb the hill when they brought the boat back. He turned on his seat to view the island; it looked magnificent in the morning sun. Turning back, he rowed toward the eastern shore to look for willow trees, but there were none along the steep rocky bluffs. As they neared the island, he turned north to where they wanted to fish.

Ralph selected a spot among some scattered weeds where he dropped the anchor. Fishing in Orchard Lake offered a new experience. When they fished in Union Lake on the edge of the drop-off they couldn't see the bottom or their bait. Orchard Lake had clear water and they could see the spinner flashing in the water. An hour later, they hadn't seen any fish nor were there any strikes. Jimmy said, "Let's move closer to the shore."

Ralph started to pull the anchor up when his pole moved. Jimmy yelled, "You've got a strike, grab the pole!"

He pulled up on the pole severely bending the tip. "It's a big one." A bass jumped fifteen feet from the boat. "Get the net Jimmy. If the fish hits the boat I'll lose him." Ralph knew the procedure, as he went hand over hand to the tip of the pole and grabbed the line with both hands. His effort created slack in the line and the bass jumped again closer to the boat. Ralph yelled, "Did you see him jump?"

"I sure did. He looks like a big one."

His hands were shaking, and the line cut into his fingers, but Ralph was determined to land the bass without the help of his friend. He slowly advanced the line wrapping it around his left hand. "He's heading your way. Don't miss him."

Jimmy leaned over the side of the boat but missed the bass on his first try. He regrouped grabbing the side of the boat with his left hand while swiping the net toward the fish. He thought he had missed a second time when the weight of the fish stretched his right arm." I've got him." Ralph had caught his first large mouth bass--- about twelve inches long.

"I done it Jimmy, I caught a bass. Give me the net."

Jimmy had his pole braced under the seat and the pole jerked downward. "I've got a strike!" Jimmy handed the net to Ralph and grabbed the pole. "Get your fish out of the net." Jimmy raised the pole to set the hook. He was ready when the fish jumped and moved the pole to keep tension on the line. After placing the pole in the water, he wrapped the line around his left hand and leaned forward on his knees to guide the fish toward Ralph. "Are you ready? He's coming your way.

"I'm ready." Using his left hand, Ralph netted the fish. As he reached with his right hand to secure his grip, he dropped the net. The net and fish disappeared under the boat. Jimmy had started to unwind the line from his hand and he gave a quick jerk to retrieve his fish. It was still hooked and he could feel the added weight of the net, but he didn't loosen his grip on the line.

Ralph looked shocked as he tried to talk. "I'mmmmm sorry, I lost the net and your fish."

"I don't think so; the fish is tangled in the net. When I pull the line up, you can grab the net." The net prevented the fish from fighting and Jimmy soon had both in easy reach. Ralph breathed a sigh of relief as he grabbed the net.

He removed the fish saying, "Your bass looks bigger than mine, but its small compared to the one you caught last summer. I can't believe it; we caught two bass in five minutes. Mr. Marohn was right about the spinner attracting fish. We caught your fish with the boat moving. Let's try trolling closer to the shore."

"My hands are shaking and my heart is still pounding. There's something about big bass and winning our bet that makes me nervous."

They trolled for another hour along the north shore. While they were fishing, Jimmy searched the shoreline for willow trees. There were birches and maples, but no willow trees. "I'm going to row around the corner and we can have lunch on the island."

"The man said to stay off the island. You said last summer you were never going to trespass again!"

"Who's going to catch us? There's no one on the island and we're the only boat on the lake. I've never been on a real island and neither have you."

"Look at all those bushes; the mosquitoes will eat us alive."

"We can wear our sweatshirts and I have some mosquito repellent."

Ralph said, "It would be neat if we found an artifact. An artifact is something from a different culture that's very old. I read that in National Geographic."

When the boat turned the corner to head south, they spotted a peaceful cove not visible from the road. Graceful white birch trees with large maple trees in the background bordered a sandy beach amongst the rocky bluffs and rugged shoreline.

Jimmy said, "There used to be a farm on the island. I'll bet the kids watered the animals here."

Ralph replied, "This looks like a good place to swim. I'll fasten the stringer to the back of the boat, and then we can go swimming."

"Good idea, we should swim before lunch." The boys had their trunks on whenever they fished and often went swimming before cleaning their catch.

## Chapter Sixteen

# Exploring the Island

After lunch, the boys donned their sweatshirts and applied mosquito repellent. They were ready to explore the island. Wanting to look for willow trees, Jimmy said, "Let's walk along the shoreline to the old house. We can explore the middle of the island on the way back." They made their way through the trees to the south shore and found the remains of the burnt house. A large chimney, not visible from the water, dominated the scene. A cluster of vines grew from the oven area where the women once cooked the family's meals.

Jimmy said, "They lived just like the people in 'Little House on the Prairie'. No electricity for lights or an oven."

Ralph remarked, "There wasn't a radio or phone and they needed a boat to go shopping. I wonder if they had a car parked on the shore."

"Without electricity they couldn't listen to a radio. The kids missed Jack Benny and all those Sunday night programs."

"I'm glad we live where we do," replied Ralph. "This would've been a tough life for kids our age, nothing but chores!"

Jimmy wondered aloud, "Where did the kids go to school? There are ten to twelve weeks you can't use a boat or walk on the ice. Maybe their mom taught them."

"If you were sick, how would the doctor get here?" Ralph hesitated, "It would be neat to talk with the kids who grew up here."

"We'll never know, but we better get going. I have papers to deliver." There were two willow trees near the water, but neither was Y-shaped. They were the only willow trees that Jimmy had seen. To make sure his effort wasn't in vain, he climbed a large maple tree to view the entire island. Willow trees grew close to the water's edge and they were easy to spot with their light green leaves, but there were none in sight. Only the south shore offered the soft moist soil that willow trees needed to flourish. The rest of the shoreline was either rocky or sandy and better suited for birches and maple trees.

The island crested in the middle and Ralph discovered a trail leading away from the house to the center of the island. He wanted to find an arrowhead or anything resembling an artifact. Brush and vines covered parts of the trail and the ground next to the trail, but his small stature allowed him to squeeze between and under the bushes while digging between them. A funny looking stone caught his eye. "I found a stone that looks like a hatchet head!"

"Take a stick and dig around, there may be more." Jimmy took a stick and started to dig on the other side of the path. Ralph stumbled out of the bushes. His hands were scratched, but he had a smile on his face. "Wait 'til the guys see these. I found two arrowheads next to the hatchet head."

Jimmy examined the find. The stones had been chiseled to a point and there were small grooves where they were attached to the shaft. "I think you're right. These are arrowheads and this one looks like a hatchet head!"

At the end of the trail the boys turned right toward the water. They encountered more brush, entwined with vines that provided an excellent breeding ground for mosquitoes. Jimmy kept busy ducking branches and slapping mosquitoes as Ralph worked his way through the underbrush looking for more artifacts. He caught his foot on a vine when something shiny caught his eye. What he found surprised him. "You're not going to believe me. There's a bone and a watch. It looks like a ladies watch."

Jimmy thought Ralph was pulling his leg. "Dig some more, maybe you can find the rest of the body."

"That's creepy. You do it."

Jimmy had his doubts. "I'm too big to crawl in there. Look around, a bunch of old bones can't hurt you."

Ralph pushed aside the brush to uncover a skull. He shuddered and stepped away. "Do you want the skull?"

"Stop kidding me." He worked his way through the brush to take a look. "You found a skull."

"That's what I said."

"I don't think we should fool around with a skeleton."

"Are we just going to leave it here?"

Jimmy remembered a story he had read. The detective said not to move a body if you found it accidentally. "Don't move anything."

"Are you crazy? Why would I touch a skeleton?"

"The man at the boat rental can call the Sheriff. I'll tie my handkerchief to this bush to mark the spot. The shiny watch will help them find the body. I've seen enough of this island. Let's get back to the boat."

As they were moving through the brush, two deer bolted across their path spooking Ralph. When he jumped out of the way, he fell backwards on his rear end. "What was that?"

"Two deer tried to stomp on you. My brother said there were deer, but you can't see them in all this brush. They're good swimmers."

"It's your turn to be in front; they scared the heck out of me."

Jimmy led the way back to the boat. He had thoroughly searched the island for the Y-shaped willow tree, and it wasn't there. He had run out of islands to explore.

The man at the boat rental greeted them when they docked the boat. Jimmy and Ralph explained their discovery as the man listened intently to their story. When the boys had finished, he picked up the phone. "We better call the Sheriff."

The boys could tell from the phone conversation that the Sheriff was on his way.

The man hung up the phone and smiled. "You boys had quite a day. When your boat disappeared, I knew you were going on the island. Nobody pays attention to the signs. Did you find anything else?"

Ralph showed the man the hatchet head and arrowheads. "These were together."

"You did well. How will you divide the three items?"

Jimmy said, "I get an arrowhead and Ralph keeps the rest. He found them."

"Those are a couple of nice bass. You boys should be proud of yourselves. There are some darn good fishermen who rent boats on a regular basis, and they don't always catch fish. I'll clean your fish and pack them in ice. Your father can pick them up. The ice costs a quarter." The man handed Jimmy a quarter. "Here's your refund for the life jackets, I deducted for the ice. You weren't wearing your life jackets when you docked the boat. Good advice is hard to follow. That's why people drown when something unexpected happens. You might want to remember that."

The Sheriff's Deputy arrived in a pickup truck. Not in uniform, he showed the boys his identification. "I live in Keego Harbor and the Sheriff asked me to take the case on my day off. The Sheriff said you found a skeleton. I need to hear the full story."

Ralph had found the skeleton. It was his story.

After Ralph finished, the deputy said, "We need to recover the remains. Can you tell me where they're located?" He handed Jimmy a map of the island.

"Go to the south shore where the home is located and follow the trail going north. We turned right at the end of the trail."

Ralph remarked, "I went about twenty feet before I found the skeleton."

"I left my handkerchief tied to the bush and there's a watch that's kind of shiny. We broke a good trail. I think you can follow it."

The Sheriff's Deputy examined the map. "Good work. You boys can head for home."

"It's getting late and I have my paper route. We won't get home in time if we ride our bikes."

"That's not a problem. I'll throw your gear and bicycles in the back of the truck and take you home."

"They caught a couple of nice bass. I'll put them in the truck. Don't worry boys; I'll tell Jimmy's father what happened."

For Jimmy, there wasn't time to climb the steep hill overlooking Apple Island. Maybe next year they could come back and explore the surrounding shores of Orchard Lake and Pine Lake. Maybe Chief Pontiac spent time at Union Lake or Long Lake, but no one he knew had ever found an arrowhead.

On the drive home, the Sheriff's Deputy asked them not to discuss what had happened with their friends. He didn't want a bunch of people trespassing on the island. He explained this to Jimmy's mother and Mrs. Williams.

After the Deputy left, Ralph slapped Jimmy on the shoulder. "Going fishing today tops everything we've ever done. Nothing beats catching a bass and finding a skeleton the same day."

"You can say that again. I thought delivering papers in the snow and those people swearing at me were the worst days of my life. There had to be something better. You forgot the big turtle.

"More fun for you than me. We haven't seen a big turtle this summer."

"I still dream about that turtle, but in my dreams I never catch her."

"I know what you mean. When I dream of the pond and those bloodsuckers, I can't get them off."

On Wednesday, the front page of the Pontiac Daily Press featured the story but made no mention of who discovered the remains. The body had been there for years and appeared to be a woman in her thirties. The Sheriff's Department needed to check dental records for a positive identification.

## Chapter Seventeen

# Discovery

On Thursday morning of the same week, Jimmy had finished cutting Mrs. Jones' lawn and she offered him a glass of milk and peanut butter cookies. She'd read the story in the paper about the Oakland County Sheriff recovering the body on Apple Island and it piqued her interest." I recall reading about a man's wife disappearing, and he lived on Orchard Lake. I'm sure it was ten years ago or longer. He probably killed her and hid the body on the island. That's something that no good son-in-law of mine would do. He lived in your neighborhood before he disappeared."

"I thought you said he left Michigan in nineteen thirty-two, before your daughter divorced him. My family moved here in nineteen thirty-six."

"Didn't you say something about fishing in Orchard Lake on Monday? Were you there when they discovered the body?"

"No ma'am. Ralph and I caught a couple of bass in the morning. The island is posted 'NO TRESPASSING'. We had our bikes and started home at one o'clock. My dad picked up the fish and our gear. They must have found the body later in the afternoon. Thank you for the milk and cookies."

He couldn't tell Mrs. Jones that Ralph and he had found the body. It made little difference that Ed Bates lived in his neighborhood. There weren't any islands in Long Lake, Cooley Lake, or Union Lake, and the money wasn't on Cedar Island or Apple Island. He had exhausted the obvious places to look but he still wasn't ready to share the letter with his family.

As Jimmy left, he waved at Mrs. Green coming down the driveway and she almost dropped her plate of cookies waving back.

"Wait a minute Jimmy and have a cookie."

"No thank you Mrs. Green, I'm behind schedule and I just ate three peanut butter cookies."

"You're still growing; a couple more won't hurt you."

He braked his bike, "I'll put a couple in my bag and eat them after dinner."

"No young boy should turn down a chocolate chip cookie."

The cookies were still warm, and Jimmy devoured both of them. "Thanks, you make good cookies. I'll see you Saturday when I cut the lawn."

Mrs. Jones came down the driveway, "That looks like a fresh batch of cookies Martha. I'll have one if you don't mind."

"I was hoping to catch Jimmy while they were still warm."

"Let's go to the porch where we can be comfortable and talk."

"Good idea. I read something you may be interested in."

Mrs. Jones poured two cups of coffee and helped herself to a cookie. "That's looks like an old newspaper. Is there something I've missed?"

"You might have read this story and didn't mention it, but I doubt it. I was throwing away some old papers and came across it. A man named Ed Bates shot at two policemen when he tried to rob a grocery store in Pontiac. He got away before they could catch him. Wasn't your former son-in-law named Bates?"

"I didn't see the story; it must have been in the back of the paper. His name was Ed Bates, and the police were after him when he skipped town in 1932 and headed to California. What my daughter saw in that man I'll never know. Back then, the police said he and Tommy McMahon robbed two restaurants where they worked as bartenders. The judge put Tommy in jail for ten years and he came here last month after he got out of prison looking for Ed Bates."

"What did he want from you? He must have known that Ed Bates wasn't here unless he read the article."

"He said Ed Bates was here in April and he tried to rob a grocery store in Pontiac. Tommy thought there was money in an old trunk that Bates left with my daughter. She in turn left it with me when she moved to Chicago in nineteen thirty-four. When Ralph and Jimmy cleaned the garage they found $75 in the trunk. Tommy said he needed money to go to Florida and make a new start. I gave him $50, everyone deserves a second chance. I just got a postcard from him; he's in Frostproof, Florida working in a citrus orchard."

"That's quite a story. According to the paper, Ed Bates was here in April. When did the boys clean your garage?"

"Right after Jimmy started delivering the paper, the first week in April. After they cleaned the garage I heard strange noises one night. I told Jimmy and he checked the garage, everything was just as he had left it."

"Ed Bates being here and the strange noises are no coincidence; he probably came back for the money. I know that criminals leave money and extra clothes stashed for a quick get away. He didn't need the money and whatever else was in the trunk in nineteen thirty-two, but he needed it now. Ed Bates is long gone by now; the newspaper article had an accurate description of him. It read like it came from a driver's license, height, weight and color of eyes and hair."

"I think you're right Martha, but its better that he doesn't have the $75. Someday Ed Bates will get what he deserves; he's too dumb not to get caught."

"This is old news, but it's better if you call the Pontiac Police. You may have information that could lead to his arrest. I read detective stories, and small snippets of information can add up and catch the criminal."

"I'll do that right after you leave. You make wonderful chocolate chip cookies."

"Thank you for the compliment, I'll make another batch next month if I can get my hands on some more chocolate chips. They're scarcer than sugar."

## Chapter Eighteen

# Back to School

Jimmy and his classmates returned to Union Lake School for the sixth grade in a brand new classroom. The teacher spent considerable time the first day reminding the class that carving initials in a new desk was forbidden. Her remarks didn't have a lasting impression on Max; he had purchased a new knife to leave his mark on the classroom. The school district had converted the old business office into a small library. A wall map of Oakland County was prominently displayed. Jimmy carefully studied the new map, but it didn't offer any additional clues. Several lakes had pointes similar to Union Lake, but none had an island. The Y-shaped willow could have been on Cedar Island or Apple Island and been cut down or fallen in a storm. Neighbors removed old trees and trees along the water were frequently struck by lightning. A large maple in the neighbor's yard came down in a wind storm when he was eight.

After he finished his paper route, Jimmy went to the basement to look at the letter and the newspaper article. There were only the two clues, an island and a Y-shaped willow tree. If Tommy Mc Mahon needed a map to find the island, Ed Bates would have put one in the envelope. He smacked himself on the forehead. Ed Bates had written the letter twelve years ago. Tommy couldn't have found the money, he never received the letter. The detective said cases remained closed unless someone found new evidence. No one would be looking for Ed Bates after five or six years and he probably returned for the money. The article and letter were tucked in the bag and returned to their hiding place. The pursuit and intrigue were over. The island would evermore be in his thoughts, but the treasure forever safe from his grasp. *I need to set this aside and concentrate on my grades.*

# Chapter Nineteen
## Surprise, Surprise

On a sunny Saturday in early October, Jimmy headed for home after finishing his route. His father greeted him and remarked that Hugh and several friends were busy building a duck blind on 'the island.' "I'm looking forward to some roasted duck."

A confused Jimmy asked, "What island?"

"The one connected to the privilege lot on Long Lake. You and Ralph dig worms and play there all the time."

"Everyone calls it 'the island,' but it's not an island."

"It was an island years ago when the water level was higher. The lagoon, where the dock stands used to be a canal connected to the lake. Twenty-five years ago a small bridge connected 'the island' to the shoreline. As the lake level receded, the canal dried up and the bridge fell apart before we moved here. Ever since

I can remember, everyone calls it 'the island.' Mr. Snow said water covered 'the island' when he was a boy. He was ninety and he died five years ago. I remember coming here as a boy with your grandfather and you didn't walk on 'the island,' it was too mucky. It's part of the privilege lot, but the community doesn't try to improve it. That willow tree I sketched for you is on 'the island.' I remembered the tree, but forgot where I'd seen it."

Jimmy took time to reflect. All the kids called it 'the island' and a willow tree marked the point. Mrs. Jones said Ed Bates lived in the neighborhood. 'The island' and the Y-shaped willow tree were two blocks from his house. The letter said he buried the money on 'the island,' and that's why the island didn't have a name.

Jimmy said, "I'm going to 'the island' to learn how to build a duck blind."

Hugh and his friends were using old branches and brush to build a duck blind to the left of the Y-shaped willow tree. They were also building a bench to sit on while waiting for the ducks. The tree bordered the water's edge and the money was probably buried on this side of the tree. He remembered the newspaper article was written in March. The ground might have been partially frozen, but under the frost line the dirt would be soft and easy to dig. The duck blind wouldn't interfere with the search. *I'll come back tomorrow after lunch.*

After helping Iris with the dishes, Jimmy took the bag from its hiding place and emptied the contents on the table. He needed to examine the clues a final time to satisfy his own curiosity. The article was dated March 21, 1932. If Ed Bates waited a week before burying the money most of the frost had left the ground by that time. In the movies he'd seen, bad guys hid when the cops chased them----then came out of hiding when they felt safe. *Ed Bates waited a couple of years and came back for the money. There's no reason to get to get my hopes up.* He looked at the secret letter that Bates left in the trunk. Sometimes people plan to do things, forget to do them, and think they've done them. *My mother does that all the time.* Maybe Ed Bates thought he mailed the letter and thinks Tommy McMahon has the money. The Shadow was one of his favorite radio programs and he loved the opening. "Who knows what evil lurks in the minds of men, the Shadow knows." *I'll know tomorrow if I don't jump out of my skin before then.* Frequently, while delivering papers he would fantasize on how the money would be spent after he found it. *If I find the money, I'll bury it someplace else and spend it when I'm older. I'll buy a car when I graduate from school and move to Seattle. From Seattle I could go to Alaska.*

That night, after hours of tossing and turning, he fell into a deep sleep. In his dream he sat handcuffed to a chair watching the Sheriff's Deputy count the money. The deputy said,

"I'm going to tell your parents that you've been a bad boy Jimmy, a really bad boy."

Later that night he woke up in a cold sweat.

A tired and anxious Jimmy got up at seven to caddy on Sunday morning. The damp foggy weather discouraged any golfers and Jimmy headed for home before lunch. Ralph stood in the driveway waiting for him. They had planned to go to the Archery Show at Commerce Township. Jimmy complained of being tired and he wasn't lying.

Ralph looked disappointed. "You said you were going, I don't want to go alone."

"Get Core to go. You can use my bike."

"Core wants to go and he can use Joe's bike. I'll use your bike."

After a quick lunch, Jimmy grabbed a shovel and with King at his heels, ran to 'the island.' With a heart ready to burst, he stood in front of the tree for what seemed to be an eternity. After several deep breaths he regained his composure. *I've been waiting six months for this, I can do it. I'll start digging left of the tree.* To his dismay, the old willow tree had many roots making it difficult to dig. *I should have brought an ax.* He removed his leather gloves to dig between the roots with his bare hands. After thirty minutes of digging using his hands and the shovel, he hadn't found the box left of the tree, or in front of the tree. He had found some worms, but fishing season ended in September.

A large root to the right of the tree divided the ground, and he decided to dig on the lake side of the root. After twenty minutes of digging on his hands and knees, he stopped to rest. *The money isn't here.* Not as easily discouraged, King started digging under the large root. Within the minute, the dog had discovered something and his nails were making a scraping sound as he tried to uncover it. He backed up to bark at the unseen object. Jimmy knelt beside King to get a better look. Reaching under the root his hand struck a solid object that wasn't another root. He stopped to wipe the sweat from his forehead while taking several deep breaths. *Could this be the treasure?* After carefully removing the surrounding dirt he grabbed the end of a small box. Slowly the box and remnants of the oil cloth were removed. The oaken box had withstood the rigors of the years and inside the box were envelopes with stacks of bills wrapped in layers of waxed paper. Jimmy yelled; "I found it!" The reaction spooked King and he started to bark. Jimmy hugged the dog to settle him down.

There wasn't a bag for the money, and it wouldn't fit in his pockets. To solve the problem, he put the money back in the box. The ground near the tree needed to be restored. He filled the holes while tamping the loose earth with the back of the shovel. Remembering a scene from a western movie, he took a branch and brushed the area to remove any signs of his digging. Not satisfied with the effort, some loose twigs and leaves were gathered to scatter around the tree. Once sure no one could detect the digging, he picked up the shovel and box to head for home. With his mind focused on the treasure, it never occurred to him that most of 'the island' had been dug up by fishermen looking for worms.

He arrived home to an empty house; the family had gone to visit his grandparents. Jimmy took the box to the basement to count the money. After separating the bills by denomination, he carefully counted the money; it totaled $741. To be sure, a second count proceeded with the same outcome. It's "finder's keepers, loser's weepers," buried treasure belongs to the person who dug it up. With shaking hands he put the money in the box and placed the box in the storage area. Turning from his treasure, he thought, *I won't spend the money until I graduate from High School.* Walking up the stairs he murmured, "I'm going to name 'the island' Treasure Island."

## Chapter Twenty

# Next Month

Jimmy sat listening to the radio news report on Sunday night. The reporter predicted snow by Thanksgiving. The weather report brought back bad memories of the April snowstorm and trudging through the snow and mud to deliver his route. Mr. West greeted him when he picked up the papers. He thanked Jimmy for doing a good job. "Regardless of the weather, people need their newspaper to stay informed."

Soon the ground would be frozen, but Jimmy hadn't buried the treasure. Every time he went for the money, something interrupted him. *I know I'm doing the right thing, so why haven't I buried the money?*

He asked Mr. West. "If I found $50 on the side of the road, should I keep it?"

"Did you keep it? You're not the first boy to ask that question?"

"I kept it!"

"Do you feel good about keeping something that's not yours?"

"No sir! I found the money last month. I planned to bury the money and spend it when I graduate from High School. I still haven't buried the money."

"We all have a conscience Jimmy and your conscience is speaking to you. You're an honest boy and it's against your nature to take what's not yours. "You'll be able to sleep better if you give the money to the Sheriff's Office." Your past will always be a part of you."

He looked Jimmy in the eye, **"What you do as a boy stays with you the rest of your life."**

"Thank you Mr. West. I feel better already."

"Remember Jimmy, rain or snow, the paper gets delivered."

"I won't let you down."

After dinner, Jimmy said he needed to share a secret with the family. He went to the basement and returned with the money. His brother couldn't believe he'd kept the secret for six months. The family agreed they should call the Sheriff. The following day his mother called the Sheriff's Deputy Jimmy had met when he discovered the skeleton on Apple Island. The deputy came to the house to question Jimmy. After counting it, he handed Jimmy a receipt for the money. "They don't have to, but the restaurants will probably give you a reward for returning their stolen property." The detective smiled, "You were on Apple Island looking for the Y-shaped willow tree?"

Jimmy nodded his head. "I looked everywhere for that Y-shaped willow tree."

"Did you look on Cedar Island?"

"I looked on Cedar Island and on Wolverine Lake."

"You should consider a career as a Police Officer. You have the makings of a good detective."

"Ralph and I dug worms and played on 'the island' since we were seven. We were digging worms there all summer and I must have looked at the willow tree ten times. If my father hadn't mentioned my brother and the duck blind, I never would've looked there."

"You were ahead of the curve when you rented the boat. After Cedar Island, Apple Island was the logical place to look. I doubt anyone would have looked on Long Lake after seventeen years. The detective assigned to the case retired in 1939. We're a small department. Once a case is closed, it isn't reopened unless someone provides new information. You were persistent, and that's the hallmark of a good detective."

"I think the kids will say it was dumb luck."

"The Sheriff received a letter from the sister of the woman

you found on Apple Island. She wanted the Sheriff to thank you for finding the body and bringing closure for the family. It means a lot to the loved ones if the remains are properly buried. With your help, we closed two old cases in six months. I doubt if something like this will ever occur again, but next time call the Sheriff's Office."

"I didn't find the skeleton, Ralph did. He was off the path looking for artifacts when he saw the watch. I'll tell Ralph about the thank you, but it would mean a lot to him if you told those people he found the skeleton. He deserves as much credit as I do."

"I'll stop at Ralph's house to say thank you from the family. If you're thinking of a career in law enforcement, come see me and I'll give you a recommendation."

"Thank you; I might do that when I finish school."

Jimmy was famous. The story made the front page of the Pontiac Daily Press, and the evening radio news mentioned him by name. The restaurants gave him $120 for returning the money and free dinners for his family. Ralph and Mrs. Jones had stated they wanted no part of the contents from the trunk, but Jimmy felt obligated to offer them some of the reward money.

The next day the boys were walking to the store on Union Lake Road and stopped at the willow tree to skip stones. Whatever their endeavor, they had their eye on the ground looking for the perfect stone. Ralph had a stone almost two inches in diameter and less than one half inch thick. A little big, but it looked to be a good stone. "Take a look at this stone Jimmy; I'm going to beat your record after a couple of warm-up throws."

Jimmy eyed the stone; maybe Ralph could beat his record of nine skips. "Where did you get that stone?"

"Janice found it picking flowers in the garden." Ralph picked up a large stone from the side of the road and threw it to warm up his arm. "After two more practice throws I'll be ready." On the second throw, he skipped a stone five times. He took the perfect stone from his pocket and tested several grips. The throw required a firm grip to achieve the needed speed for ten skips. After several swipes of his arm, he knew the stone was too big and he couldn't get a comfortable grip. He looked the other way to consider his options. *I could try it, but I can't get a good grip. On second thought, I could wait 'til next summer, when my hands are larger to set the record. Someday I'll have a growth spurt, Jimmy has one every year.* What to do?

Jimmy sensed his dilemma. "You'll never find another stone like that one. Why don't you wait 'til next summer when your hands are bigger?"

"That's what I was thinking."

"Why waste a good stone."

"Thanks for telling the Sheriff's Deputy to stop at the house. My brothers couldn't believe it when the deputy knocked on the door. He said without my help they wouldn't have solved the case. People ignore me because I'm small, but being small has an advantage sometimes."

"There's no way a larger person would have found that skeleton."

"We were working together cleaning Mrs. Jones garage and you were with me on Apple Island. You should get some of the reward money."

"There's nothing in the trunk that I want." Ralph looked at Jimmy and remembered the day they emptied the trunk. "You figured out the clues and did all the work."

"I'm giving thirty dollars to my parents, thirty dollars to Mrs. Jones, and thirty dollars to you. Do you think that's fair?"

"Wow!!!! What will I do with thirty dollars?" Ralph stopped talking to think. "That's really fair, but I owe you a dollar. You paid for everything when we went fishing at Orchard Lake."

"If it makes you feel better it's okay with me." Jimmy handed Ralph thirty dollars. "We're rich! I can get an Almond Joy and you can get a Mounds Bar."

"The next time my dad goes to Pontiac; I'm going to get new hockey skates and hockey gloves. I'll wait 'til spring to get a new bike." He pocketed the money and smacked Jimmy on the shoulder. "You did the right thing when you gave the money to the Sheriff. It was an awful lot of money, but it wasn't yours."

"It kept me awake for a couple of weeks. After talking with Mr. West, I figured out that stolen money isn't buried treasure. If I kept the money it was the same as stealing. Mr. West didn't know about the money, but I remember what he told me."

***"What you do as a boy stays with you the rest of your life."***

# Epilogue

For readers interested in history, I've provided a brief description of the area where the story takes place. The fishing site in the 1940's had a substantial parking lot east of Union Lake Road that has been washed away with time. The lake hasn't changed and the Michigan Interactive has a detailed picture of Union Lake that shows its many depths.

'The island' (part of the privilege lot on Long Lake) referred to in the book is now a lovely park enjoyed by the neighborhood. Morey's Golf Course (reopened as the Union Lake Golf Course) is currently located south of Wise Road and west of Union Lake Road. In the 1940's the fourth and sixteenth holes bordered Long Lake and the course was north of Wise Road and west of Union Lake Road. During the war (1943 to 1945) Jimmy caddied at Wise's Golf Course. The course was 4,900 yards long, there were no par five holes, and par for the course was sixty five. A pond on the dreaded par three third hole captured many errant tee shots. The Morey family purchased the golf course after the war in 1946.

In 1944, Union Lake Village had two grocery stores and a gas station. The locals called it a village, but residents of Oakland

County, renown for its 358 lakes, identified with a lake. Jimmy and Ralph were from Union Lake, a schoolmate lived at Round Lake, and there were twin sisters from Lower Middle Straits Lake. Union Lake Village and the surrounding villages were part of Commerce Township. If the lake had a nearby gas station or grocery store, the residents referred to it as a village. The lakes appeared on the map, but not the villages. (In 2011 there are sixty lakes in the Oakland County that are not named and referred to as 'No Name Lakes.') Three lakes surrounded Union Lake Village. Cooley Lake was to the Northwest, Long Lake to the Southwest, and Union Lake to the Southeast. The Long Lake Jimmy and Ralph swam in was the largest of the five Long Lakes in Oakland County. Residents living near a lake, but not on the lake had access to the nearby lake through local privilege lots. Accessible rights to use the privilege lots were recorded in property deeds. Jimmy's family and Ralph's family lived in a double privilege subdivision with access to Long Lake and Union Lake. Jimmy's family docked their boat on the south end of the bay at privilege lot one on Union Lake. Across the bay the state of Michigan owned and managed a fishing site. Unlike the local privilege lots, this fishing site offered public access to Union Lake allowing fishermen and boaters to launch boats and park their vehicles.

Unlike many of the neighboring lakes, Union Lake had depths from very shallow on the eastern shore to a depth of

110 feet at the center of the lake. A drop-off was dangerously close to the western shoreline where a swimmer could go from water neck high to well over his head in one stride. On the south shore a swimmer could dive off the bank into five feet of water. Because of the lake's depth, cold water, and steep drop-offs, many fish and turtles grew to extraordinary sizes. The cold springs feeding the lake produced an overflow controlled by a small dam that released water into a stream running into Long Lake. Union Lake didn't lose water during the summer drought.

The smallest of the three lakes, Cooley Lake, had varied depths. Both the eastern and western bays had shallow bottoms choked with weeds that hampered boating and swimming. In the summer the water level could drop one to two feet, shrinking the usable part of the lake. Half the size of Union Lake, Long Lake's shallow bottom limited the use of the lake. Summer droughts often dropped the lake level one to two feet turning two bays into mucky goo. In July and August homeowners on the eastern shoreline had docks with no water beneath them and boats sitting on the mud with no access to the usable part of the lake. Plans were progressing to pump out Long Lake to remove the sediment and muck when the war ended. The majority of homes on the three lakes were summer cottages owned by people from Detroit or Highland Park. The population of Union Lake more than doubled in the summer months when the cottages were occupied.

World War II had changed life at Union Lake and the surrounding communities. In a show of patriotism, many homes and businesses displayed an American Flag and everyone talked about the war. The adults were busy working in the defense factories in nearby Pontiac and had little time for fishing and boating. The essentials required for daily living were rationed, from gasoline and tires, to meat and sugar. Ration coupons were needed to buy rationed items, and the School Boards were responsible for issuing them. Jimmy's mother picked up her coupons at the Union Lake School. If a family ran out of sugar coupons toward the end of the month, they would borrow a cup of sugar from a neighbor until they received next month's allotment. The federal government had imposed a thirty-five mile an hour speed limit on all roads to conserve gasoline. Jimmy's father, a commercial artist worked for the Burroughs Corporation in Detroit and the reduced speed limit added thirty minutes to his daily trip. His father carpooled with four other men to conserve gasoline and reduce wear and tear on their tires and cars. The reduced speed limit and gasoline rationing discouraged people from Detroit and Highland Park from frequent trips. Many families waited until the Fourth of July holiday before opening their cottages.

Most of the boys and some of the girls graduating from

high school joined the Army or the Navy. Some lost their lives fighting in Europe or the Pacific, and were featured on the front page of the newspaper Jimmy delivered. The war began when Jimmy was eight, and he had few memories of life before the war.

Jimmy and Ralph would row for hours exploring Union Lake and dropping the anchor to check the depth. To their surprise, it took three fifty-foot ropes to reach the bottom in the middle of the lake. Union Lake had many good sized Leatherback Turtles. You could spot the Leatherbacks by their pointed nose when they surfaced for air. They were strong swimmers with large front and rear flippers. Year around residents respected the powerful jaws of the Leatherback and referred to them as snapping turtles. Last summer Jimmy spotted a huge Leatherback Turtle sunning its back at the fishing site and he spent the summer trying to catch it.

Mr. Marohn, the shopkeeper, and a man in his late fifties, said the big turtles had been there since he was a small boy. "Union Lake is different Jimmy. Every thing grows bigger in the cooler water, and most people using the lake have never seen a big Leatherback Turtle or caught a large Northern Pike. Years ago my uncle caught a Northern Pike forty-two inches long. He claimed to be fishing in eighty feet of water. I don't know if anybody keeps records on who's caught the biggest fish, but I've never seen a larger pike. A Northern Pike speared in the winter or caught in the summer is three feet or smaller."

People from the city considered country folks to be somewhat backwards, but that didn't bother Jimmy and his friends. They loved living at Union Lake where everyone knew their neighbors and there was always something to do. In the summer they played baseball, went fishing, caught frogs, and swam every day. On summer nights, the kids from six years old to early teens played 'hide and go seek.' In the winter the boys and girls cleared the ice on Union Lake for skating, and the boys cleared a separate area on Long Lake to play hockey. Most of the kids tobogganed or sledded down nearby Foley's Hill. During the winter months, the fishermen used the fishing site to drive their cars onto Union Lake. They cut holes in the ice and either fished for or speared Northern Pike and large bass. Some of the pike were three feet long, the biggest fish Jimmy had ever seen. A few fishermen had ice shanties with wood burning stoves to stay warm while they fished. The shanties approximated four feet by six feet, enough space for a hole in the ice, the stove, and a couple of chairs for the fishermen. On a winter weekend in January or February, one could see three or four cars parked on the ice with smoke curling upward from the assortment of metal chimneys that decorated the roofs of the shanties.

# About the Author

Jim Haskin and his wife Alice are retired from the office products industry and reside in the Bellevue, Washington. They have five married daughters and thirteen grandchildren also residing in Washington State. Their home overlooks Kelsey Creek, a salmon stream that passes through their back yard. Jim spends his time writing, caring for his yard and playing golf. In the fall the family looks forward to watching the returning salmon that navigate the creek.

His two books, 'Jimmy and the Big Turtle' and 'Jimmy and the Secret Letter', tell the story of life during World War II for two boys growing up at Union Lake, Michigan.

CPSIA information can be obtained at www.ICGtesting.com
Printed in the USA
BVOW010537160911

271365BV00002B/12/P